The Lilac Autumn

A Life Story By
Cecilia Weidner

Dolores West

This book is dedicated to my Vince and my Tina without whom I would not have made it through the darkness.

I stand in eternal awe of the women of Africa who never stop to smile, never think themselves too mighty and important to go down to a child's level to play and to be merry, despite the greatest hardship humans have to bear on this earth. To their eternal love and dedication to their grandchildren, their incredible spirit and perseverance I dedicate this story.

I.

Majestic cumulus clouds with stark white edges and a pale apricot tinge drift lazily across a deep blue sky. The blueness of the sky made the edges seem even more pronounced. Laying on one's back and looking at the sky, the clouds looked like generous helpings of freshly beaten meringue, slowly drifting by.

There was a slight breeze that caused the pale lilac flowers to fall down from the jacaranda trees in what resembled the closest thing to purple rain. The entire driveway was coated with these flowers despite the fact that Phineas swept it just this morning. By the way, Phineas was my gardener.

Later today there will be a thunderstorm—at least that was what the weatherman predicted. A magnificent spectacle of nature played out almost every other afternoon during the summer here on the Highveld.

How rude of me, here I am going off, and I have not even introduced myself. I am Lillian Johnston, Lilly to those in my inner circle. This is my home, here in the northern suburbs of Johannesburg. It has been my home for the last twenty odd years. When I married Chris and we bought this property, this area was classified as "comfortably in the mink-and-manure belt." This is an uppity way to say "wealthy suburbs," to the north of the city's centre, on a ridge facing north into Africa.

I was standing in my entrance hall. Under foot was a magnificent Tabriz carpet in all the shades of pink—wool and silk on wool—for those in the know and now you know too. It lay on top of rosewood parquet I chose more than twenty years ago. This beautiful wood reflected the pink shades woven into the carpet. It definitely created the "wow" effect I wanted when I chose it. Over all these many years, many friends and friends of the children have walked over this beautiful wooden floor, leaving the marks behind that told the story of lives being lived.

You see, I liked detail. I liked to know what everyone wore at a dinner party as well as what colour polish the ladies wore on their toenails and if their heels were smooth or not. Well, don't you do the same? When you see a woman beautifully dressed with sandals, don't you look to her heels to see if the polish reaches everywhere? I just liked to know the whole story, to see the picture in its entirety.

I checked my image in the large gilded mirror that hung in my entrance hall, exactly as I always did. In a few minutes I would leave to go to one of my famous ladies' lunches. As the society photographers were always on the lookout for a picture at the country club, one simply had to look one's best when going there.

My friends and I got together at the country club once a month. One cannot simply apply for membership there, you know, one has to be introduced or suggested to the board as a likely candidate and then invited to apply. One had to be aware of the circles one moved in. This club was very old, very distinguished, and very moneyed with excellent security. These were all very important factors in my world, you understand.

These get-togethers were really very necessary. My friends and I caught up on gossip, we checked who had gained weight, which brand of shoes were being worn and by whom, and we networked amongst ourselves on behalf of our husbands. Many a deal, which our husbands later finalized, originated at our women's lunches. At these lunches one listened carefully, then, during the course of a quiet dinner or a pre-dinner drink with the husband, one casually mentioned what one had learned via the grapevine and sometimes straight from the horse's mouth. Over the years one learned exactly how to present these facts so it appeared perfectly incidental, and then one lets her husband do his thing. Of course one was clever enough to never refer to this fact—no, one made it appear as though one was very surprised when the very issue one had discussed days or weeks before actually materialized as a clinched deal! My, oh, my, we all had such clever husbands!

Every single one of those ladies, who attended that day, was married. Our husbands were businessmen. In the fishpond which was and still is, the business community in Johannesburg, everyone knew everyone else. Strong contributors to the economy of this country. Business leaders, the lot of them. Real pillars of society and fathers of the nation. Strong principled men.

I was just about to take my purse when the gate bell rang.

"It is all right, Selina. I will get it," I called up the staircase. Selina was our domestic worker. It is a serious misnomer as she was so much more, but according to the law, she was classified as a domestic worker.

In Johannesburg it was a common occurrence to have strangers ring the gate bell or doorbell. We often had these incidents where strangers rang the bell. They collected money (they did not really accept anything else, mind you) for very many charities. Most of these charities did not actually exist and some existed but never received any of the funds that had been collected.

We had cameras on all four corners of the walls surrounding our property, so I checked the television screen of this closed circuit in my kitchen, fully expecting to see someone there with a book and a bag. Instead, I saw a slight woman with a small child on her hip. Over her shoulder she carried a huge bag with painted elephants.

"Can I help you?" I asked into the intercom, at the same time checking my Rolex, as I had to be going soon or else I was going to be late for my lunch.

"Madame Johnston?" I was taken aback because Johnston was not written on the letterbox or on the intercom at the gate. We were not in any telephone book nor could one get our address or phone numbers from the telephone information service. The voice was soft and she spoke with an accent. I did not know this person at the gate and nobody told me they would be sending someone around to my house.

"I'm afraid I don't know you. How can I help you?" I was a bit irritated and it shone through in my voice.

"Madame Johnston, I need to urgently speak with you," Her voice sounded shaky, out-of-breath. She had an accent and she had a baby on the hip. I did not see any movement in the street except for a gardener mowing the lawn two houses down the road. One had to be careful of robbers here where I live. This was Johannesburg in the twentieth century. Gangster's Paradise as it said on the number plates of the cars.

I pressed the button to open the gate. Why? I cannot tell you to this day. Maybe it was because she had a baby with her. Somehow I always think that mothers who have borne children cannot be murderers. A person who knew how hard it was to give life, will automatically have respect for it; a mother simply cannot take life away. A mother knows to nurture it. To treasure the tiny flame which we call life.

I walked out onto my terrace with the wrought iron balustrade around it. I walked to stand under the flowering wisteria from where I could observe the progress of this woman and child down my driveway toward me. The sun was shining, the birds were singing and life was good. Just another perfect day in Africa.

She was slight, actually, painfully thin. She was looking around, either watching out for dogs or admiring my garden. From the way she was turning her head around, I would bet she was watching out for a dog. She wore a white dress and it looked like she was about to collapse under the combined weight of the baby and the bag over her shoulder.

From the corner of my eye I could see Phineas. He was planting petunias in the far corner of the garden. He dug the spade into the ground, put his foot on it and decided to take a break.

He slowly took out his pipe and tobacco. He was seldom without the pipe hanging from the corner of his mouth. When I told him about the dangers of smoking, he told me that the stench of the smoke kept the flies and no-see-ums away. How could one beat such logic?

He was also looking at this woman and child coming down the driveway. He took out the tobacco, stuffed the pipe and lit it. He puffed on it. Sometimes I got impatient with Phineas because he seemed to do everything in slow motion. When I told him this, he laughed and told me that I should slow down. "Meddim, you have no taxi to catch," he said to me, "we are in Africa." It was the truth anyway.

The electric gates swung silently shut. Phineas must have been wondering who this unknown black woman with the small child was. Well, we would all know soon enough.

She reached the bottom of the steps that led up to the terrace and I went to help her. Her breathing was laboured and the perspiration was pouring down her face. She dropped the bag on the ground as I reached her.

The little child kept its head on the woman's shoulder whilst looking up at me with large black eyes. The little one was dressed in white as well with white socks. The socks had a lacy frill at the top, but the little one was not wearing shoes. The socks were still white underneath so the baby must be very young, I thought. It did not appear as though she could yet walk.

So there we stood at the bottom of the steps to my terrace, both of us looking at the other and I finally took charge of the situation.

"So how can I help you?" *You have come this far and this is quite far enough, thank you*, I thought to myself.

This young woman fixed her gaze on me and it made me feel uneasy. She did not answer. Instead, she ascended the stairs slowly, holding onto the railing at the side. I had no choice but to follow. She climbed the stairs slowly, like someone who was very advanced in years. She was holding onto the baby on her hip for dear life, almost clutching the little one to her. I made up the rear, carrying the huge bag, which, by the way, was rather heavy.

At the top of the stairs she turned toward me. She put out her hand. I took it but her handshake was limp. No pressure. No sign of vitality. I looked down on her head. Her features were really quite petite. She had beautiful long fingers and her fingernails were short. Her hand felt surprisingly cold, considering that it was rather warm and her face was covered with perspiration.

Here we stood at the top of the ten stairs, on my patio with the cream-coloured, handmade Italian tiles, surrounded by a garden filled with exquisitely smelling flowers in the warm African sunshine.

She dropped her hand to her side. "My name is Ayanda Kambilu."

"Pleased to meet you," I said in response. "You already know who I am." An uneasy silence descended on us, except for the hadida shouting somewhere in the garden. This bird, the hadida, has the reputation for announcing imminent disaster in almost all folkloric tales in Africa.

"Let us have a seat over there," I said, indicating the seating area with the overstuffed patio furniture. I had these chairs specially made as I liked wide chairs with armrests—one could spend the entire day curled up in such a chair with a book. I had spent many a night reclining in one of these chairs listening to friends talking, discussing politics as though one could find the answers to all the problems in this world during a single evening.

She sat down in the appointed chair. The little child shyly looked at me and then buried its face under Ayanda's arm.

"Would you like something to drink?" I stood while I asked her this.

"Yes, please, a glass of water." The nervousness had not left her voice and from the way she spoke I could hear that her mouth must have been very dry.

I walked into my kitchen and I caught a glimpse of the clock on the wall. I was by now seriously late for my lunch.

"Who is out there?" Selina looked at me questioningly. She had been with my family for decades. She had been like a grandmother to my children. That is why they call her "Gogo." She was cleaning upstairs and must have witnessed Ayanda's arrival from an upstairs window. Nothing, absolutely nothing, happened in my household without Selina knowing about it.

"Her name is Ayanda, but who she is and what she wants, I don't know."

Gogo looked at me for a while, then she said, "Lilly, you know the crime is bad. She is maybe a spy for the tsotsis. How can you open the gate just like that?" She indignantly placed her hand on her hip. "Maybe they are waiting outside right now."

"Calm down, Gogo. Nothing will happen. She is very weak and she has a child with her. Maybe she is collecting for some charity. Could you please bring us a tray with water and two glasses? Oh yes, please bring some juice for the baby." I turned around and walked back toward the patio.

The little child had climbed down by now and was standing next to Ayanda's chair with her little hand placed on Ayanda's knee.

I sat down opposite them. We were sitting under the wisteria with the bunches of purple and white flowers softly blowing in the breeze above us, spreading their delicate scent in the air all around us.

I smiled a put-you-at-ease smile at the young woman. Nervousness emanated from her. My lunch date was, at this stage, a thing of the past. The girls must have been wondering where I was because I absolutely never missed our lunches. I had heard my mobile ring a couple of times but I could not get to it because of my visitor.

I leaned forward across the glass coffee table and spoke to the baby. "What is your name, little one?" She just stared at me with her large black eyes and buried her head in Ayanda's lap.

Ayanda answered my question. "Her name is Sophie. She understands only French. She is now sixteen months old." Ayanda had a soft smile around the lips. She looked up at me. "Sophie is my daughter." She picked Sophie up onto her lap.

So the accent was French. We sat for a moment in silence. The birds were singing. In the distance someone was still mowing the lawn. The beautiful clouds were drawing together in the sky above us. The clusters getting bigger. There was definitely going to be a downpour later. Everything was so incredibly normal.

On the patio was a very uneasy silence. I could feel that Ayanda wanted to say something. I could also feel that she didn't know how or where to start.

At that moment Selina arrived with the tray. I poured a glass of water and placed it in front of Ayanda. I handed the cup with the juice to Sophie. She must have been extremely thirsty because she immediately took it from me and started to drink. Little rivulets of berry juice ran down the corners of Sophie's mouth and dripped onto the white dress. It made me smile to see the little one enjoying it so much.

I looked at my Rolex oyster watch on my wrist. I placed my arms on my knees in order to support myself as I leaned forward.

"Ayanda, what can I do for you? If you don't mind, I actually have to be going because I am already quite late for an appointment."

My left arm with the watch and the tanzanite and diamond ring on my ring finger was perfectly displayed in this position. I saw Ayanda staring at my hand, and then she lifted her eyes up to meet mine.

She looked me straight in the eyes. "I know your husband." A statement.

I waited for her to continue and then I said, "Many people know my husband, Ayanda." I smiled a Madonna kind-of-smile. Indulgent. Proud. Satisfied. Christian Johnston, Chris to almost everybody, he was an easygoing kind of guy, was rather well known. He was a director of a mining corporation with interests all over the world. I had been with him on some of his business travels, as much as my social schedule and commitments concerning our boys would allow me to, mind you. The travel schedule was hectic what with work as well as social engagements, meeting with people who were of importance and those who could possibly help to roll a stumbling block out of one's way in some of the countries.

Ayanda looked down at Sophie on her lap. She placed her arms around the little girl and rested her chin on the crown of Sophie's head. Her eyes were downcast and her voice was soft, "I *really* know your husband." She hesitated, "He is Sophie's father." Her voice was barely audible as she said this.

At first I did not understand what she was saying. The words seemed to come out single and unattached to one another, not as part of a sentence. There passed a period of silence, how long I cannot say, it felt very long. I felt quite nauseous and at a loss for words for hearing this horrible information.

"Ayanda," my voice had become quite cold, "you suddenly appear here on my doorstep out of the blue sky, from God-knows-where, to tell me to my face my husband fathered a child with you." There was a slither of steel in my voice. "I am sorry for Sophie if she does not have a father but that does not make my husband her father." I sat up straight and put my arms on the armrests of the chair.

Silence had descended on my patio once again. This time it was a heavy, sticky one. Somewhere in the garden a hadida called again, the bad omen in Africa.

"Mrs. Johnston," her voice was very shaky and soft, "please believe me. Chris is the father of Sophie. I can understand you must be terribly shocked. Please believe me I am very, very sorry to do this to you. If it were not for the circumstance you would never have known about Sophie." Her voice trailed away.

My legs had gone numb and I could not get up even if I wanted to. I looked at the little girl sitting on her mother's lap. Now that I scrutinized her, I noticed that her skin colour was very much paler than that of her mother's. There was nothing in her features that suggested Chris was her father. I tried to remember the faces of my own three sons when they were babies. My imagination failed me. I could not find a resemblance.

I simply sat there with my back against the backrest, my arms on the armrests, my hands hanging at the end of my arms, and my feet supported by the tiles beneath it. I could not come up with a question or a statement. Seizing this moment, Ayanda started to speak.

"I come from Cameroon. I worked there for a mining company."

She spoke slowly and softly with her French accent. She looked up at me and our eyes locked. Two large tears dammed up in her eyes, flowed over, and slowly started to roll down her cheeks, down to the pronounced jawline and then dripped down to find a final resting place on top of Sophie's head. It did not take long for her cheeks to be completely wet with tears. She hugged the little one very close to her, almost like a ragdoll.

I waited for her to continue. "I was the executive assistant to the manager of the operation in Cameroon. I had a lot to do with Chris..." She turned her head away and looked toward my rose garden.

"Mrs. Johnston, I have found out that I have AIDS. Sophie is infected too. Chris might be infected as well." If I thought this scenario could not get any worse, then I was sadly mistaken. It just did.

Ayanda looked at me with anxious eyes. I could not find a single word to say to her. It felt like I had been kicked in the stomach, and I ceased to breathe. I had gone icy cold. I closed my eyes in order to shut out all this in front of me.

I just sat there with closed eyes. My mind refused to take in these horrid words that this woman had just spoken.

Ayanda continued with an unstable voice, large tears rolling down a river over her ebony cheeks. "I have brought Sophie here to you. With her father she has a chance to survive. I cannot afford the care she will need to stay alive. I am dying and there will be no one to take care of her once I am gone." She buried her face in Sophie's neck and in a broken voice she whispered to the little one. I assumed it was a prayer because I heard the word "*Dieu*" a few times.

The next instant she got up quickly and thrusted Sophie onto my lap. She turned around and practically ran down the steps, sobbing as though her heart was breaking. I sat there utterly stunned. For someone who had absolutely no energy, she moved incredibly fast.

She took a shortcut across the lawn. I frantically looked around for Phineas but he must have gone outside the gate to the street. I noticed too late that the pedestrian gate was held open by the big rock we usually placed in the way to keep it open. Before I could take any action, she reached the gate and she was gone.

Sophie slid down from my lap and started to crawl as fast as she could toward the stairs in order to follow her mother. At this stage the little one was consumed with heart wrenching sobs.

Even if I wanted to, I could do nothing. I was without energy, nailed to my chair.

As though ordered by divine intervention, Selina appeared on the patio. She must have heard the cacophony and come to investigate. She raced forward and reached Sophie in the same instant as Sophie reached the top of the stairs. She scooped the hysterical baby up in her arms and turned to me.

"Who is this child? Where is the mother?"

"I don't know, Gog." My voice was flat. I spoke softly, "I don't know."

Then I noticed the big bag Ayanda carried over her shoulder. She had left it by the side of her chair. Selina disappeared into the house with Sophie. I got up to fetch the bag. A little voice from somewhere told me I would find answers in that bag. I returned to my chair, as I did not feel strong enough to open this bag whilst standing.

I lifted the flap and pulled the zipper. Inside was an assortment of baby clothes, a couple of diapers, and an envelope. White. Sealed. My name was written on it in small, girlish handwriting.

I pulled it out of the bag and tore it open. I hoped to find the answer to this insanity in this envelope. Inside I found three A4 sheets neatly folded. I proceeded to fold the sheets of paper open on the coffee table. The first one was a vaccination certificate. The following was a baptism certificate: Sophie Marie Kambilu, Catholic like Chris, myself, and our sons. The last one was a birth certificate. I quickly scanned over the page, all written in French. The father's name was Christian Johnston. At that moment everything turned black in front of me and there was a deafening screeching sound in my ears. I fainted for the first time in my life.

For how long I remained in this unconscious state, I do not know. I eventually came to my senses, and I was still alone on the patio. No sign of Selina or Phineas. A good thing too there had been no one to witness this scene. I have never lost control in my life! I have never been unconscious. What a horrid thought. Though slightly disoriented, I was ashamed.

My luncheon! Heavens! I looked at my watch. I was now more than an hour late! I was just about to get back on my feet when I caught sight of all the papers scattered at my feet. I frowned. *Why are there these papers? Oh no! Chris. Ayanda. Sophie. Dear God, it cannot be. Please let it not be. Please help me.* My scattered thoughts rose through my confused mind in a frenzy.

Inside the bag were two more envelopes. Small ones. Both sealed.

One was addressed to me. The other was addressed to Sophie.

I carelessly ripped the one addressed to me open and started to read.

> Dear Madame Johnston,
>
> I do not know you personally but I have heard a lot about you from Chris. He spoke very highly of you. He told me about your work with children who are HIV positive. He said how brave he thought you were for taking in these children, that you took care of them while they waited to be placed in a home. He said you work tirelessly to

ensure they have the medicines and the
care they needed to survive.

I was furious. I wondered at what stage of their intimacy they
made time to discuss me. How dare he discuss me with someone
he was screwing! The mere thought hurt so much I felt sick again.
I continued to read.

> I am coming to you without Chris knowing.
> He also does not know about Sophie.
>
> *Alors*, I met Chris at a company function
> three years ago. It was in Douala. I was
> new to the company. Chris was very kind
> to me and talked to me about my job.
> He always asked how I was doing.
>
> I was so excited to get a job with such a
> big company. I went to France to study
> and immediately found this job when I
> returned to Cameroon. In my country
> there is great unemployment and, pardon,
> madam, poverty you will not understand.

I looked up over the page into my garden. *How can she think I
do not understand? One cannot live in Africa and not be confronted with
this crippling poverty all the time. It is in your face at all times.* I looked
down again at the paper in my hands. Part of me wanted to stop
but another part told me to continue.

> I offered to show Chris around after
> work one day and it simply happened.
> We did not have a relationship in any
> other way.

13

When I found out that I was pregnant
I resigned. I left and went to live with
relatives. I never saw or heard from
Chris again.

I learned I was HIV positive while I was
pregnant. I had no access to a doctor
when I gave birth. Sophie was born
naturally. She is also infected.

I am a mother and I love Sophie more
than life, madam. You are also a mother,
and you can understand this. I cannot
keep my baby alive. Chris spoke very
admiringly of you. He said that you are
a woman of great compassion. He told
me about your charity work for children
with AIDS. He said that you love
children, and that you are a wonderful
mother yourself.

I am very ill, madam. I have a short time
left in this life. I am going home to die.
Please take care of my Sophie and let
her live. I know that you will.

May God bless you. I am forever in
your debt.

Ayanda Kambilu

I sat there stunned, silent, and speechless. Inside me all the
emotions were thrown together in a maelstrom with a million butterflies hovering in my solar plexus so that I was breathless.

I did not know how I felt, confused, certainly. I just sat there,
existing. Rationalizing. Trying to bring order to my thoughts.

Yes, Chris travelled a lot and he certainly must have met many
people on these travels. Yes, there were many women in his world.

Beautiful and exotic and clever. But he is my husband, for God's sake! Knowing many women, working with them, and socializing, certainly, does not mean he would have children with them. Or could it be? Was it possible that this young lady, I say young because she is at least twenty years younger than me, had something so special Chris lost his head? That he became so attracted to her that he was prepared to sacrifice the sanctity of our marriage?

Just then the ringing of my mobile phone interrupted my thoughts. It was a catchy, modern tune which, under normal circumstances, never failed to make me happy: a tune from my youth which I enjoyed hearing. My fifteen-year-old son was responsible for putting this ringtone on my phone. But today this tune did nothing to make me feel happy. The upbeat tone sounded perfectly out of place, considering the circumstances.

I went to fetch it from my handbag in the hall and looked at the display. It was Chris.

"Hello." My voice was flat.

"Hello, gorgeous. Are you at lunch?"

Silence on my side, then "No." I cleared my throat.

"Lilly, what's wrong, babe? You sound strange."

"Yes." I kept quiet after this one word.

"Lil, are you still there?" I could hear the worry in his voice now. He probably thought I had been hijacked. Unfortunately such things happened on a regular basis here in this city.

"I'm here, Chris. I think you had better come home right away. There is a crisis here." Having said this, I did not wait for him to respond. I simply put the phone down.

I could not move from my chair on the terrace. I felt so very tired, and I wanted to cry. Being lost in thought like this I only noticed that Selina was standing next to my chair when she started to speak. She had little Sophie secured on her back with a huge pale pink bath sheet held together in the front with a diaper pin. In Africa the women carry their little ones around like this. The baby will be secured on the back with a blanket or a towel and stay on the back for the longest time. This way the mother could do her chores without having to watch the little one and the little one was as close to the mother as possible. The mothers sung to the little ones and talked to them, and it was most conducive to catch a nap whilst sitting on the back. The movement of the mother lulled the little one to sleep. This method made for very happy babies.

As I looked at her I wondered where she could have possibly found the diaper pin. My boys were all grown now. No such things as diaper pins around any more. Diapers had become sophisticated these days and no longer required pins.

Sophie was quiet. She was chewing on a piece of bread.

"Lilly, the baby is hungry, and she needs to be cleaned up."

"Take her down, Selina. I will clean her up right here."

I looked in the big bag Ayanda left behind for a clean diaper. Selina just stood there looking at me and I avoided her gaze.

I held out my hands so I could take Sophie from her.

"Lilly, did the mother bring her here herself? Did she just drop her and leave?"

"Yes, Selina. You can say that that was the way it happened." I purposefully avoided her gaze.

Selina shook her head from side to side, clicking her tongue and muttering something under her breath. Her coming to her own conclusion had saved me from a horrifying explanation that I could not presently fathom how to formulate.

I took care of Sophie and handed her back to Selina. She swung her onto her back again with ease and a rhythm that never failed to amaze me. The way an African mama has with a child just cannot be taught to any other childminder. I know from the experience with my own children that Sophie will be asleep in no time.

The revving of a car engine in front of the gate interrupted my thoughts. The next instant the gates started to open and there appeared my husband in his powerful German SUV, screeching down the driveway.

II.

From where I was, I saw Chris looking at me. I sat on the terrace as I had done so many times in the past when he came home. The scene looked the same right now. It looked normal. The gardener was working in the garden, planting flowers, birds were singing in the trees. Me, the gracious wife, sat on the terrace waiting for her husband.

He got out of his car and slammed the door with a loud thud. I cringed because the door would have closed by itself if given a slight push. My husband seemed to have forgotten that fact just now.

I looked at him approaching the house. He was a fabulous specimen to behold. Tall and dark with the physique of a runner. He was very sporty, my husband. He ran marathons. He said the solitude of the open road gave him time to contemplate and to think about all he had to think about but did not have time for during his normal busy day. He said many solutions to business situations came to him whilst running. When he pounded the open road, there were no distractions. Just him, the wind, and the road and his body went into overdrive. The human machine: the most spectacular design ever.

How far will you have to run to solve this problem, darling? I wondered as I sat there watching him ascend the steps to the terrace two steps at a time.

"Hey," he said as he reached me, bent down, and kissed me on the head. "What's wrong, Lilly? You look like you have seen a ghost?" He sat down opposite me. He sat on the edge of the over-stuffed couch with a curious and inquisitive look on his face. His hands reached out for mine across the coffee table.

I did not stretch my hands out to him. I looked at him. I looked down. I moved deeper into my seat and I crossed my arms over my chest. I sat up straight because it felt as though there was a very heavy weight atop my chest and I had difficulty breathing. Finally I cleared my throat and I looked him in the eye.

"I had a visitor this morning," I paused and looked at him, "a young woman called Ayanda Kambilu." I kept my tone flat whilst carefully observing his reaction.

There was no sign of recognition in his eyes. He looked at me questioningly. "So? Who is she?"

"You apparently know her, Chris …" My voice trailed off. I could see it in his eyes how his mind was racing. There was silence between us. Then recognition of the name dawned in his beautiful black-brown eyes. "I have met only one person with that name. She was from Cameroon. Working for the company over there." He said it softly.

"Yes. Well, this very same Ayanda Kambilu felt it necessary to pay me a visit." I looked at him and I wondered what he might be thinking of at this moment.

"What did she want?" He leaned back in his seat. His hands were resting on his thighs, he seemed very relaxed and unsuspecting. I looked at those hands with the long tapered fingers, the neat square fingernails. He had the hands of a pianist, my husband. As I was staring at his hands I wondered how they caressed this other woman. Did he do to her what he did to me with those hands?

I kept quiet whilst trying to breathe normally. I felt as though my heart was pounding in my throat and that somehow he could hear and see this.

"She brought us your daughter." Silence. At first he did not even seem to understand what I have just told him.

"My what?" The last word was said in staccato mode. His voice sounded strangled, incredulous.

"You heard me. Your... daughter." Despite the warmth of this beautiful early afternoon, I felt as though I were freezing. In fact, I had to control myself or my teeth would have started rattling.

"Lillian, how can you allow a complete stranger to dump a child on you and just believe that it is mine?" He was standing now, looking down at me. I could not look him in the eye so I simply stared past him at my garden.

"Chris, I don't know what to believe. I need to hear it from you." Now I raised my eyes up to him. My voice was soft. "Do you know this Kambilu woman?"

"Yes! But that does not make me the father of her child!" He leaned across the table and took my hands in his.

"Did you sleep with her?" I asked this quietly. Something was strangling me and I had trouble to force my voice past this huge blockage in my throat.

He looked at me for the longest time and then he looked away. He threw his hands in the air and then slowly raked his fingers through his mob of dark, curly hair. He got up and walked a few steps away. He put his hands in his pockets. A lock of hair fell back across his forehead. I looked at him and, as always, I was touched by his handsomeness. He walked away from me to the side of the terrace. It looked as though he wanted to escape but there was a wrought iron railing all the way around the terrace. "There's no escape, Chris. Answer the question, please." My voice was unsteady and hoarse.

I sat quietly and waited for him to return to the couch because that was the only thing left for him to do under the circumstances.

"Lillian..." He stood in front of me and then he sat down on the edge of the coffee table.

I looked him straight in the eye and then I leaned forward. "Did you sleep with her, Chris?" I asked again. Softly.

I felt his eyes on me. The silence, which descended upon us, seemed as though it lasted an eternity, as though we simply were caught and frozen in this heavy silent bubble. I felt suspended, as if the picture in this horror film were frozen for a period of time that felt like forever.

"Let me explain." He reached out for my hands, and I desperately reached for his. I was so praying that all of this was a terrible, dreadful misunderstanding. His hands were warm and strong and reassuring and his fingers stroked over mine slowly and calmingly.

"Lillian…I…yes, I did. I did have sex with Ayanda."

What could I say?

What could I do?

Where could I go?

Where could I look?

How could I continue living after this?

There was total and utter confusion written on my face. In a moment like this, one could do absolutely nothing. So, I did nothing. I just sat there, looking at him. Then I closed my eyes as though to shut out the world and, therefore, reality. In my mind's eye, thousands of conversations we have had, visions of him with our sons, images of him staring at me across a room full of people, images of us together making love played like a movie.

I have been betrayed, for God's sake. I have been betrayed and my wonderful perfect marriage compromised in a way that hurt me mortally. I felt like I was going to die. Me, who could counsel friends for hours after they found out their husbands' infidelities! It had to happen to me! I always thought my world was perfect.

I have always thought of myself as a very principled person. I took the vows I made when I married Chris very seriously. I always have. I never strayed because Chris meant everything to me. We belonged together. "In sickness and in health, for better for worse, till death us do part…" Does anybody really truly understand the immense meaning of these words? Does anyone really contemplate that when the dizziness of being in love has gone—disappears as it surely will—the vows which had been taken during the abnormal state of "being in love" were still very much valid? Do people understand the responsibility each partner carries with regards to respect and honesty in a marriage? One partner to another? Marriage is a contract, which is not understood by most of the people entering into it. The implication of placing one's signature at the bottom of that document is so momentous that when the difficulties arrive on the scene, most partners try to get out of this sacred bond. This has always been my sincere belief … and now?

Chris and I have three sons, and, by the grace of God, I still have them. Connor was twenty years old at the time and at university in England. Christopher was seventeen and at boarding school in the beautiful, rural hills of Kwazulu Natal. At fifteen, Christian, Jr. was the youngest. He was at a private boys' preparatory school in Johannesburg and the only one of our boys still living at home. Even though my family was spread out all over the world, we remained incredibly close to one another with regular phone calls and visits. I often spoke to my boys, and I knew everything a mother should know about their lives. At least, I liked to think that I did. I was the one who kept Chris up to date on what was going on in the lives of his sons, because the boys and I had been mostly on our own. Chris had been working all over the world for a mining corporation he joined straight after he completed university studies.

I had an unusually close relationship with my boys. I have shared their successes and their failures, and I have secretly cried when a dream had been shattered. I was present at the side of the sports field, cheering them on, shouting like a demented person whenever they played a cricket match and their team was winning or they scored runs, or they been chosen for the first league swim team. I was their biggest fan. I have shared the trials and tribulations of the first girlfriends of my two older boys. In short, I was a mother in the true sense of the word. I am still, to this day, their fiercest supporter and will not tolerate anyone scolding them or saying a bad word about them. I will defend my boys like a tigress, and even though I know their shortcomings, I will never admit to anyone that they have a single one.

Me, as a wife, well, I would have liked to think I had done everything in my power to be as close to perfect as any husband might possibly demand. I am very well groomed, always have been. I trained with a personal trainer. I swam daily at the gym because this exercised muscles in other ways altogether. I never, ever walked around in easy clothes because it looked sloppy. Besides, what if guests would have arrived unannounced? I just could not bear the thought to ever have been caught off-guard. I had to be in control, in full command of my world.

All this I did because I considered it my duty toward my husband. So he could be proud of me. So he did not have to go snooping around for some floozy or fast sex as so many of my friends' husbands did these days. I did it so that Chris wanted to come home in the evening or from a business trip. To keep the excitement alive between us. To keep the dynamics of the very complicated relationship between a husband and a wife, perfectly in order.

I firmly believed, all these years, that if I was a wonderful mistress, if I was the proverbial lady in the lounge and the whore in the bedroom, then my husband would not stray. No matter how delectable the provocation, no matter how exotic the temptation.

I am educated. I could hold my own in a room full of intellectuals, and I could be silly and lightheaded when needed. By God! Was I wrong? How could everything I ever believed in have been so far off the pitch?

I sat there quietly looking at Chris. No, I scrutinized him, silently. I tried to comprehend where I went wrong. What could I have done to make my gorgeous husband stray off the path of righteousness and virtue? How did I force my husband, the love of my life, to find sex with another woman? Did I neglect him?

Were there times I was too preoccupied? I feverishly searched my memory for clues but I came up with blanks.

All this time, silent tears rolled down my cheeks. Chris still sat on the edge of the coffee table looking at me. He had always been helpless whenever I cried. He had always been at a complete loss for words on such rare occasions, I should say. He placed his hands on my knees. Slowly caressing. Slow circles going up the outside of my thighs, usually it was the beginning of something else but I just could not. I wanted to throw up.

"Lilly," he said my name softly, like a caress, his voice deep and velvet. Usually it made me weak in the knees when he said my name like that. My tears continued like a silent waterfall coming from deep within me. As I sat there looking at Chris looking at me, I became aware of a pain so deep and intense that it felt as though there were another entity living inside me. I felt my heart contract and it felt like the life was being squeezed from me. I feared that I was having a heart attack.

I kicked off my shoes and pulled up my legs, hugging myself with my forehead resting on my knees. This pain inside me knocked the air out of me, and I gasped for breath. Silent sobs racked my body.

I did not realize for how long we sat like that. Chris did not make an attempt to console me or hold me. Nothing. I locked him out.

When the tears finally stopped, I looked up. My cheeks were wet and my mascara smeared all over my face. My silk blouse was soaking wet across my breasts, the silk sticking to my skin.

The pain inside me was real. I felt raw. Chris looked at me. He looked concerned. His cheeks were also wet, and he had loosened his tie.

"Lillian."

"Chris." We both spoke at the same time.

"Chris, there is something else." I looked at him and I took a deep, slow gulp of air in order to deliver the final blow.

"Ayanda," I swallowed, "Ayanda has AIDS. Sophie has it too. Ayanda said that you might be infected as well."

All colour drained from his face. The skin over his cheekbones became totally pale and only the darkness of his beard shimmered through. He stared at me. He opened his mouth but no sound was forthcoming.

I was suddenly furious. I wanted to physically attack him. I wanted to pound his chest and scream at him. I wanted to slap his face and cause him to hurt like I was hurting.

I jumped up, my body shaking with fury.

"How could you, Chris? How could you fuck around in the first place? How could you endanger your life? By what right could you endanger my life? Do I mean so little to you? How about your sons? Our sons, for God's sake, Chris! How could you do this to us? What have I done, what have we done, to deserve this?" I was livid.

I could not bear it to be near him another second so I turned my back on him and started toward the front door.

"Lilly, I can explain."

I turned around and looked at him scathingly.

"Really?" sarcasm dripped from my voice.

I looked him in the eye. Repulsion clearly visible on my face.

"Forgive me if I am not interested to listen to your explanation, darling husband. Tell me, did you tell her how misunderstood you were at home, what a bitch your wife was? How deprived and neglected you were? Which one was it, Chris?"

I started to cry again, and the anguish I felt was written all over my face so I turned on my heels and disappeared into my fortress.

Selina materialized in front of me with Sophie, fast asleep now, still on her back. Selina looked first at me and then past me to where Chris was still sitting on the terrace behind me, but she did not say anything. She merely walked around me toward Chris.

I turned around to watch what was going to happen. I could see Chris's gaze going over the little one but he did not say a word. He just sat there, on the edge of the coffee table.

Selina put the glasses back on the tray and, without looking at him, picked up the tray before walking back into the house. With Sophie rhythmically moving on Selina's back, she moved past me toward the kitchen as though I did not exist.

Chris and I were meant to go away over the weekend. We had a game farm to the north of Tswane, about a three-hour drive from Johannesburg.

It was magically romantic on our farm. I'd organized the interior of the house as well as the design of the farmstead with the assistance of one of the leading design firms in Johannesburg. This farm was our hideaway where we went to get back to nature and to get away from it all. We sometimes took our closest friends along but mostly we went alone or with the boys when they were home. Christopher, our middle son, especially loved it because he was allowed to ride motorbike and quad bike and sleep under the stars.

But this weekend we would have been alone.

Just the two of us, celebrating the way we were before our sons were born. You see, it was our twenty-fourth wedding anniversary. It would have been very special. Just the two of us. Christian had arranged to stay with a friend for the weekend.

Instead of standing in my rose garden on the farm, here I was. Standing at the window of my bedroom staring out over my city garden toward the horizon to the north. Night was falling. The sky was changing colour. The huge dome which constitutes the sky above our heads, was almost purple toward the east, gradually changing to a pale shade of blue above my head and then into a delicate pink slightly to my left and gradually to a shade of deep orange toward the west where the sun would go to rest. It never ceased to amaze me, the spectacle of the setting sun. All the colours of the rainbow present and yet all of it fit so perfectly together. All of this happened before my eyes. Another spectacular sunset over Africa. I witnessed this every single day and I was struck by it every time. Except tonight. Tonight it left me untouched, my mind in a catastrophic turmoil.

Our house was built on a ridge looking north onto the dark, exotic continent of Africa. I stood at this very spot before drawing the velvet curtains. Every night I reflected upon how blessed I was because I was fortunate enough to be able to witness this scene before my very eyes. Tonight, I was sad, angry, and very, very afraid. The beauty outside my window left me cold.

I could not imagine my life before today. It felt as though I had never been happy. It felt as though all the things that happened before today had happened to someone else. Not to me. That was Lilly with the perfect life and now I am Lilly who might have HIV inside me. It might be coursing through my veins right now, attacking my cells. The enemy within. The virus, which presented as a friend, then destroyed everything from the inside. I might already be dying. It had been sixteen months, she said.

Lillian Johnston's life was organized. Everything in my life was arranged. I planned ahead. We were wealthy, for heaven's sake! These things did not happen to wealthy people like us or did it? I tried to do everything according to the book! Why me? I was confused and scared to death, quite literally, as a matter of fact.

What if I got that disease and I died? Who would take care of my sons? Chris, Jr. still needed a mother. He needed guidance. Everyone needed a mother, for God's sake! I realized I would drive myself over the edge with all these questions. I would go crazy with all these thoughts. I could not control them and I shuddered. I was cold.

I turned around and sank into one of the velvet covered wingback chairs near the window.

There was a knock at the door.

"Come in," I said, just barely audible. I had no strength left. I felt so exhausted.

It was Selina.

"Lilly, I made the baby some vegetables with rice. I gave her a bath. She fell asleep when I dressed her after the bath so I put her to bed in the nursery. I have prepared a bottle for when she wakes up in the night. Do you want me to sleep in the room with her?"

"Yes, Selina. I think that will be wise. Thanks."

I looked at Selina and smiled. It was a lopsided smile. I got up and crossed the room toward her. If I could I would have given her a hug. But Gogo did not like being hugged. She shied away from contact. It was only with children she was different. Her tenderness knew no end when she was with them. She was the most patient person I have ever known.

I thought of the time when my boys were born and of their childhood. Selina was there. Carrying them on her back, teaching them to walk. Teaching them rhymes and songs in her native tongue. And always there was laughter. Never a harsh word or a sign of impatience. I remember trying to teach them they had to make their beds. Selina was appalled I wanted to make boys make their own beds. She told me off in a very stern voice and told me that so long as she can still do it, she will be the one to do it, and I should leave them alone. What could I say? She was their surrogate grandmother.

When Connor was five years old, he got a bicycle for his birthday. While he was learning to ride, Gogo and I took turns to run beside him and hold up the bicycle so that he did not fall. The times he did fall she was there, cradling him in her arms saying "Sorry, sorry, sorry, sorry, *umfaan.*" I had no chance to get near him. This ritual repeated itself for Christopher as well as for Chris, Jr.

I started to cry looking at Selina standing there in my room. She cast her eyes down, embarrassed by my emotion. Pretending she did not notice so that I did not lose face in front of her.

"I will make a salad and grilled chicken. Dinner is at eight." She turned around, softly closing the door behind her.

I walked back to my chair. Tears blurring my vision, I sat back down and perused my surroundings. Sobs made my body shudder.

This room was exquisitely furnished. The chairs were so incredibly comfortable, and the bed was a king-sized beauty. Velvet at the windows, voile curtains forming a veil were held back with tassels in dazzling colours. On the table by the wingback chairs stood a vase filled with white lilies and roses. The flowers were replaced twice a week. This was something I loved to do. To be in my home. To make it beautiful. This was our refuge, a sanctuary where my husband, my children, and I could relax and let our guard down.

I served on the committees of a few charities. One especially close to my heart was a charity that cared for babies and children infected with HIV. In a country such as mine, where the need was so great, it was only fair that if one could give something back to those less privileged, they did. The unfortunate ones who seemed to exist in a twilight zone—their existence ignored by everyone.

Until now I had always been slightly detached from all the misery out there. Sure, I took in abandoned babies. Sure, I cared for them for the few days it took before they were placed in a home. I knew that by becoming attached to them, it became impossible to let them go again. Well, I took care of them with Selina's help that was. These little souls passed through my life, always in transit to a safe house, where someone else would permanently care for them. Many of these babies were found in trashcans around the city. Borne by a mother who herself was probably still a babe. Unable to feed herself, let alone another human being. Both of them infected with that horrible virus, both of them facing a horrible, dreadful, painful end, if they did not get help and medication.

The virus. It brought me back to the present. God, I might have that alien beast pulsing through my veins right then as I sat there. A time bomb ticking away inside me, just waiting for the right circumstances to rear its ugly head. The dry cough, the skin conditions, the constant situation of being ill. Oh God, please help me. I threw my head back, shut my eyes in silent prayer, and, once again, began to cry.

III.

Hi. We have already met, albeit under dreadful circumstances. I am Christian Johnston, Chris to those who know me well. I am Lillian's husband.

This is pretty much how I define myself, as Lillian's husband.

We have three sons together: Connor, Christopher, and Christian, Jr. Smart boys. Handsome young men. Because of my job I did not have much to do with raising them. That was Lilly's job. She did it much better than I could have done anyway.

Connor is at university. He wants to become a doctor. He says he wants to work for Doctors without Borders one day. He is a good kid. Always wanting to help others. Takes hundred percent after his mother.

Christopher is away at boarding school. He is at the same school I attended and where Connor also went. Christopher is really good at rugby. That boy has speed, and he is built like a brick house. Real solid. He is a bit of a wild one but his soft spot is his mother. He is fearless. I took the boys white river rafting in America last year. It just couldn't get wild enough for him. He is a rebel. Always questioning the establishment. It drives Lilly crazy sometimes the way she has to reason with Christopher.

Christian is at school here in Johannesburg. If I say so myself my namesake is really handsome. Thankfully, as yet, he is totally unaware of this fact. He is a computer freak. He seems to understand the way cordless items communicate. Computers, cell phones, play stations, you name it and Chris can operate it. He's incredible. Lilly says he communicates in a language we do not understand. He plays all kinds of sport and is really good at swimming. He has a magnificent body already now and he is only just beginning to develop.

Their love of sport the boys have from both Lilly and me. Ever since they were very little we have encouraged them to participate. Win or lose—it doesn't matter. What is important is to have fun and to be part of a team. This is what Lilly always says. I always tell them that one participates only in order to win. To come in second, means to lose. This is how I see life.

From the moment they were born, Lilly had a special bond with the boys. She has always been fiercely protective of them. Always. I never interfered in the way she educated them. I was surely in the background, and I supported her in every decision because she's smart, otherwise, I wouldn't have married her.

Of course I did all the father-son activities: rafting, bungee jumping, paragliding, surfing, and scuba diving. Once I took the boys to Moçambique to swim with whale sharks. Lilly was incensed. She said I was irresponsible and that I was endangering the lives of her sons. Never mind about me, but they're my sons too. She seems to forget that sometimes. I love them as much as she does. Only thing is I am not as eloquent as Lilly. She has an easy way with words. Not me.

"Oh, Lillian," Chris sighed deeply. He dropped his head backwards onto the backrest of his leather chair. He was sitting in his study. The walls were panelled with a dark wood, and the drapes and plush carpet were olive green. The soft lighting from the various Tiffany lamps cast a warm glow over the chairs and sofas.

Lillian had created this room for him. Opposite the bay window that overlooked the garden, stood a heavy desk made from Rhodesian partridge wood. It was behind this desk that Chris was sitting right now. Along the walls and behind him were bookshelves reaching from the floor to the ceiling, filled with all his books on minerals and mining. That was his world.

A beautiful framed map of the ancient world hung on the wall to his left. He turned his head to look at it. He remembered when they bought it. Him and Lillian. They were in London. He'd been on business, and she'd come along to shop. One afternoon she attended an auction. There she saw the map and promptly bought it.

He remembered the way she looked when she gave it to him. Like an excited little girl. He nearly had a heart attack when she told him what she paid for it. But she was so thrilled about the map, so pleased that she found something he had wanted for the longest time. He could not bring himself to be upset with her over the exorbitant price.

"Lillian, Lillian, what a woman," contemplatively he spoke to himself. He raked his fingers through his hair and massaged the muscles in his neck. His tie was hanging loose and the buttons of his shirtsleeves were undone.

I have never seen Lillian at a loss for words. Or helpless for that matter. She is always in control. If she is hurt she will never show it. I know when she has been hurt because I know her so well. She hates feeling vulnerable. She does not allow herself to feel sad. She says life is too short to waste the moments we have to be happy, by being sad.

She is like this because of her past. Lilly is an only child who lost her parents when she was very young. They were killed in a car crash and she was the only survivor. Both her parents were single children, and the grandparents were already long gone. So she was an orphan.

She does not sleep much either. She always seems to be awake when the sun is around. When we are on our game farm we always get up before the sky starts to brighten in the east. We await the sunrise sitting on the deck under the lead wood tree drinking steaming cups of homebrewed coffee watching the sun rise up in the sky and the movement of the animals coming to drink before sunrise. Mid-thought, Chris suddenly realised where he was. A shock. The present. Reality.

"Lilly is a superb wife. She is clever, witty, and sexy. What have I done? Why have I done this? How can we continue? How will things ever be the same again?" he softly questioned aloud.

Selina had rung the crystal bell three times before Lillian and Chris finally appeared for dinner.

They came down the passage toward the dining room together. Chris looked at Lilly but she stubbornly stared at the marble tiles on the floor whilst walking toward the dining room. The Persian runner on the floor in the wide passage muted their steps.

They reached the table at the same time, and each one sat down at their usual place. Like every evening. Tonight it would be only the two of them. Normally there was much chatter at the table but they had nothing to say tonight. There was just this huge vacuum between them. At the same time, it was heavy with things unsaid. Too much to say, yet no one knew how to start, much less what to say and what not to say. In the end both just kept quiet.

They served themselves and there was the clinking of the serving spoons and then silence again. This was a silence that went beyond quiet. Quiet could mean contentedness, a silent kind of happiness. This, however, was a silence with a screeching undertone.

With their appetite severely lacking, they merely pushed the food around their plates. Lilly could not stand it any longer so she pushed her chair back and left the room without saying a word. He looked at her and desperately wanted to draw her out but, from her demeanour, gathered it was best to say nothing.

Chris heard her footsteps disappear down the passage in the direction of the grand staircase that led to the bedrooms on the first floor. There was no point to remain at the table any longer so he left in the direction of his study.

The rumbling of the thunder awakened me. I turned my head to look at the clock on the bedside table. A little after one o'clock in the morning. A little more than an hour since I looked at the clock the last time. The space next to me was empty.

I pushed back the covers and walked over to the window. I opened the curtains and the majestic opera of an African thunderstorm unfolded before my eyes. The constant low rumbling with intermittent flashes of chains of lightning followed by claps so loud it felt as though the ceiling would collapse on my head any moment. Here, on the ridge, where we lived, it sounded especially loud. Must be because of all the rock. It somehow intensified the sound. The lightning lit up the dark purple mass of clouds that stretched as far as the eye could see, lightning permitting.

I opened the window to be even closer to the spectacle. The storm outside reflected my inner torment. Feelings, so violent in their intensity, disallowed me any tranquillity. There was no harmony inside me. My equilibrium was so disturbed I could not sit still in my beautiful chair. Even the grandness of this natural phenomenon, which was playing out in front of my very eyes, could not quell the torment I felt. It made me groan and squirm in the chair where I sat.

Then the wind started to blow. A huge whoosh drove the rain thundering atop the roof. The sound of the rain, the cracks of lightning, and the rumble of the storm overhead, I sat there in front of the open window and became part of this. Nature in sympathy with little old me and the potential internal catastrophe.

I did not realize for how long I sat watching the storm, eventually the worst of it moved on toward the east. All that remained was the rain. It would stay for a while until that also dried up and tomorrow morning a glorious sun will once again light up the African sky.

I was brought back to reality by a loud knock at the bedroom door. A really loud knock. I opened the door to find Selina with a squirming Sophie in her arms in front of it.

"Ssshh, sshh," Selina was trying her best to pacify the little one but to no avail. The little one wailed. I put my hand on her forehead. She was burning up with fever.

"Get dressed, Gogo. We have to take her to the hospital immediately." I took Sophie with me and put her on my bed while I quickly got dressed for the drive to the private hospital near my home.

Gogo and I left the house together with a howling Sophie on my arm. She did not want the bottle or the pacifier, and it was obvious she was in pain. Gogo got in the back of my German sports car with the little one in her arms, and I screeched down my driveway as fast as the rain would allow me.

The streets were deserted except for the guards sitting inside the little guardhouses inside the gates of the properties we passed. The effect of the storm was present everywhere with small rivers running down the sides of the roads, massive amounts of leaves and jacaranda flowers washed together in heaps on top of storm drains. No cars or even a cat out this time of the morning. Even the homeless had found a hovel to spend the night out of the way of the storm. I felt as though the three of us were alone in the city.

I ignored the flashing traffic lights, just slightly slowing down as we approached intersections. For most of the road, I kept my foot pretty much flat on the gas pedal.

At the clinic I parked my car in front of the emergency entrance. Sophie was still crying and fretting. At this stage it sounded more like a tired moan. She lay limp in my arms as I took her from Selina. Her little body must be absolutely exhausted.

I put her head on my shoulder and placed my hand protectively at the back of her head. The little arms hung limply at her sides. There weren't any tears coming out of her closed eyes. Just an incessant moan emanated from her.

We entered the reception area. Thank heavens there were no other patients there. This was a good sign. It meant we would get to see a doctor right away.

There was a male nurse sitting behind the desk filling out papers, probably administrative details on all the patients having passed through earlier in the evening. He looked at me questioningly.

"This little one is ill, and I need a doctor to see her immediately," I said fully in command. "She has AIDS."

Silently he passed me a form to fill in. Nothing said. With so many people having this dreaded disease in South Africa, it had almost become the norm to see someone suffering from AIDS. He got up from behind the desk, walked down a short passage, and disappeared through a door, which he shut behind him.

I passed Sophie to Selina and proceeded to fill out the form. After a while, the nurse came back. "The doctor will be here shortly. Please follow me." He took us through to a cubicle and drew the curtain around us. I sat on the bed with Sophie nestled against my chest. Selina stayed behind in the reception area.

We heard light footsteps coming in our direction. It was the doctor, a very attractive young black woman with a very professional demeanour.

She put on latex gloves before she turned to us.

"Are you the mother?" she asked softly as she stood in front of me.

"No," I said.

"Is she the daughter of your domestic?" she asked again.

"No," I said. "She is family."

The doctor looked at me inquiringly, probably because of the way I said it. I could see many questions flash across her face. Without further ado, she touched Sophie on the back. Softly, I lay the little one down on the bed.

The doctor turned to me finally, after having thoroughly checked Sophie through. "I will have to admit her. We have to run some tests. I have to find out how far advanced the disease is. She is quite ill, and I suspect pneumonia. We'll be able to tell for sure once we have done some blood work."

She faltered and looked down. Then she looked up at me, "Is the baby on a medical aid? The treatment can be costly and—"

"That will all be taken care of. No need to worry about the costs. I will settle the bills. Just get her to live." I used all the reserves at my disposal not to break down in tears. I looked the doctor straight in the eyes with steel in mine.

"Then let's take her through. The sooner the better." She turned on her heel and walked out of the cubicle. I picked up Sophie in my arms and followed closely behind.

Selina got up from her chair as we entered the reception. "Just wait here, Gogo. I will come back to fetch you. The doctor wants to keep Sohie here at hospital."

At the reception desk, the nurse got up after a brief discussion with the doctor and led us to the paediatric ward. Upon our arrival there, a very efficient-looking woman dressed in green overalls, a blue cap, and blue coverings over her shoes, took Sophie from me. She took Sophie through to the paediatric intensive care unit and told me to wait in the waiting area. I stood at a glass wall watching what they did with little Sophie.

The little body was limp. Only the chest moved up and down rapidly because she was breathing too fast. The fever was extremely high. Her doe-like black eyes were closed. She did not make a sound or stir as they set up the intravenous lines in her arms. They put tubes down her nose, and heart and lung monitors got hooked up to her little chest.

As I stood there at the glass window looking into this room, I could not help but to have the tears take over. Wave after wave of silent sobs clogged my throat.

There she lay. A small little person with a beautiful name, Sophie. Totally, but totally, alone in this world. Desperately ill. Abandoned by her mother. Abandoned! What kind of a mother abandoned her own child to whom she had given life after carrying that child for forty weeks below her own heart? A hard, painful process that was meant to make the mother treasure and nurture the life she had brought forth! Mothers were supposed to guard and protect their children. Not leave them on a terrace in the care of a complete and utter stranger and then run away! My mind completely shut down on this fact; it was incomprehensible as it was, this situation.

Now that I was directly involved, it was altogether harder to accept the incomprehensible. A helpless little girl who was not acknowledged by a father—a father who was responsible for her coming into this world in a moment of carelessness. A thoughtless act it was, chasing after the personal pleasure without a second thought about the possibility of what the outcome of his deed might have been.

The doctor came to me, taking off the mouth guard and the gloves as he came through the door.

"Hi. I'm Dr. Selwyn. Are you responsible for the little one?" he asked.

"I'm Lillian Johnston, and, yes, I am responsible for her." I wiped the tears off my cheeks with the back of my hands.

He stood next to me looking into the room where the nurse was still busy with Sophie. "She is very, very weak, and she is running a temperature. I cannot say anything at this stage. We will know more in the morning when we have the results of the tests."

"Will she make it through the night, doctor?" I simply had to ask this.

"I honestly don't know. We have done the best we can for now. You can go to her if you like." He glanced at me one more time and I noticed the softness and the warmth in his chocolate brown eyes. Then he walked off, out the door into the corridor.

The nurse at the station took me by the arm. "Before you can go in there you have to put on sterile clothes," she said.

Fully dressed in this sterile green protection, I reached Sophie's bed. The beautiful eyes with the long lashes were closed. Her little baby hands lay, but for a twitching of a little finger every now and then, almost lifeless next to her. Needles with tubes were attached to the back of each little hand.

I stood there hugging myself as my earliest childhood memories flashed in front of my mind's eye like a slow motion movie. I remembered when I realized I was totally and completely alone. Totally alone. No more mummy or daddy. Nobody who played afternoon games with me. No more mummy to read stories about fairies and castles before being tucked in to drift off to dreamland.

Although there were other grownups who cared, hugged, and loved me, I never felt my mama again. Her smell, the secure feeling whenever she touched me, her sweet gaze when she looked at me, the warmth in her voice when she said my name. All gone.

When I was a girl, she came to me when I had nightmares. She would climb into bed, hug me close to her body, and tell me how the angels would come riding down to earth on moonbeams. Then these angels would come into my room and they would sit at the top and the bottom of my bed. They even had names: Ella, Ingrid, Granddad, and Grandma. She banished nasty old wolves, dragons, or nightmares—nothing ugly was able to get past her godly line of defence. And so, huddled into the foetal position with my mama, I would fall asleep peacefully, without a care in the world.

Then, one day, we left in the morning and only I returned. My mommy, daddy, and I were driving in our car. They were singing and we were all laughing. Then, terrible, horrible noises, and mommy was screaming. I was very scared because I had never heard Mommy scream like that. Gone to the land of the angels, both her and my daddy, in that car crash only I survived. For the longest time, I imagined Mama riding down on a moonbeam every night to be with me. I would get up to open my curtains after I was put to bed. Then I would climb back in my bed and wait for her to come. I would whisper to myself the way my mom did. "Close your eyes, my darling. All the little angels just got onto a moonbeam down to your room to come and watch over you. Here comes Granddad and Grandma. Too many angels to count, all coming to sit here at the top and there at the bottom. Nothing can happen to you now."

I always added "Mommy" to my list of angels. Before Granddad and Grandma. Then I would hug my pillow and cry softly because she was not there. I could not feel her behind my back. Eventually I would drift off to sleep, so very alone. Right now I have that same feeling of loneliness. I could taste it even.

The noise emanating from the heart monitor pulled me back to reality. I stood there next to Sophie's bed, hugging myself. She was only sixteen months old and she was alone. She was fighting for her life. She was destitute. Left in the care of a total and complete stranger. At that moment, something changed inside of me. My thoughts became crystal clear, and, suddenly, I knew. I knew with unbelievable certainty that Sophie was my responsibility. All this had a purpose. The meaning and consequences of this purpose, I did not know as yet, but I knew. She had come across my path because there was something I had to learn, to discover about myself, our lives…something.

She was the daughter of my husband. He was the father of my sons. She shared the same blood as Connor, Christopher, and Chris, Jr. She was family. She needed me, and I would be there for her. I would fight for her, and she will live. I will haul her back from the jaws of death and do everything in my power to make her live. No child deserved to die, definitely no child who had been placed in my care.

I took a pair of latex gloves from the box next to Sophie's bed. To protect her already weakened immune system from further danger, I slowly put on the gloves. I touched her little feet. They felt terribly cold despite the warmth in the room. I could feel the chill through the gloves. I massaged the little feet with slow rotating movements, and I started to speak to her, "Close your eyes, my darling. All the little angels just got onto the next moonbeam down to your room."

I stayed with her. Talking to her, humming her songs I used to sing to my sons when they were small. As I softly sang and hummed, I became quiet inside myself. It was as if I found solace in these peaceful rhymes. Even though Sophie was so bitterly ill and could not understand me for the language barrier, the nurse seemed to think it had a calming effect. It is sometimes not what we say which makes a difference, but definitely the way in which we say it.

I went back toward my car via the emergency ward. Selina sat patiently in the chair where I had left her. Her head resting against the wall and her eyes closed.

39

I gently touched her shoulder. "Come, Gogo, let's go."

Bewildered she looked at me, then the reality of her surroundings dawned on her. "The pickaninny?"

"She is having the best care possible right now. They will let us know if there's any change." I spoke softly because the emergency ward was encapsulated in an eerie, spooky silence. The ghosts of all those who had sought help, present in the stillness.

On the way home we were both silent, each of us busy with her own thoughts. There was a new day barely breaking the blackness of the eastern sky and the hawkers were on their way to take up their positions in the city. Minibus taxis, on their way to delivering the early shift workers timely to their duty, began to crowd the roads. At certain intersections the traffic build up was evident, and there was loud hooting in the air.

I rehearsed the scene with Chris in my mind, only to realize that whatever I envisaged now, would be completely null and void, as I could not imagine how he would react. I slowly drove up my driveway, over the tracks which I had made a few hours earlier. These were not so visible anymore because of the rain and the carpet of fine purple flowers which fell down because of the storm. Chris' car was parked where he had left it the day before. The dogs lay sleeping on the terrace near the front door. It looked like just another Saturday morning before the sun came up. Peace reigned supreme in my kingdom.

Chris should be in his study, I thought as I loudly opened the front door. I walked across the entrance hall to his study. There he lay, asleep on the couch in yesterday's clothes. Unshaven and completely rumpled.

Considering the circumstances, he could not have passed a peaceful night but driven by exhaustion, must have eventually fallen asleep.

I sat down opposite him. "Chris," I said his name flatly.

He did not stir.

"Chris," I said, this time a little louder. He opened his eyes. Then he turned to look at me. He swung his feet down and dropped his head in his hands.

"Lillian?" He rubbed his face.

"Do you want some coffee?"

"Yes, please. Extra strong."

I got up to go to the kitchen to fetch each of us a cup of coffee. Upon my return, he was still sitting where I left him with his hands covering his face. I placed the cup in front of him on the low table.

"We must talk, Chris."

"I know, Lillian." Softly.

"I had to take Sophie to the clinic in the night. She is serious but stable right now. The doctors will run some tests to see how ill she really is."

He just looked at me. Those black-brown eyes quietly and intensely stared back at me. I could not read the message in them right then. Could it be uncertainty? Regret? Shame? All of these I imagined I saw in his beautiful velvet eyes, and I realized then was not the time to remind him of what he had done. I had to be positive and take the lead, to announce the way forward. I had to steer us through the present minefield, and I had to do what was right for him, for me, and for our family. It was not the time to apportion blame. There was a little girl, deathly ill, in a hospital bed, and my family was potentially falling apart. I had to cope. I had to make the decisions, as usual. Only this time, my decisions would affect not only my family, but also our entire social circle. It would affect our standing in society and change forever the way people had perceived Chris and me until now.

"Chris, Sophie has come to stay. If she makes it through the next couple of days, she will remain with our family," I said it as a statement.

"Lillian, she might not be my daughter."

I cut him off, "Don't you dare, Christian Johnston." I said it softly but with such steel and determination in my voice that he looked at me with surprise.

"You must have thought about this when you had your moments of pleasure with Sophie's mother! Now is not the time. There is a little baby girl in intensive care, fighting for her life! She has been abandoned by her mother, and I will be damned if I will allow her to be abandoned by her father as well!"

I had jumped up from my chair. I glared at him as he stared up at me.

Chris got up and walked across the room to his desk. He stood next to it with his arms folded across his chest. "What do you suggest we do, Lillian? Take her in? How do we explain her to the boys?" his voice raised.

I went to stand right in front of him. I looked him straight in the eye and with my voice low said, "Don't you raise your voice at me."

He walked over to the window, and as he opened it the smell of jasmine and purple rain filled the air. These smells always made me happy. It reminded me of the happy times, of summer. Forever after that day, it became a fragrance to remind me of deep crisis, of feeling helpless, and an awareness that I did not have control over my life.

It was unimaginable to think that only twenty-four hours ago my life was as close to perfect as one's life could get. How was it possible that it could go so wrong?

Chris, you and I have a greater problem than explaining the appearance of a little girl in our household. We, you and I, might be infected with the virus."

He looked at me. I could see the silent fury in his eyes but he looked down and said nothing.

"You and I need to be tested," I said this quietly whilst looking at him.

"Do you know what you are saying, Lillian?" he shouted with fury and anguish and fear in his eyes.

"Yes, Chris, I know exactly what I am saying. You brought this into our home, not me!" I screamed at him with a fury that wanted to break loose out of me. "We might both be infected! You were the irresponsible one, and now I have to take care of everything as is usual!"

He sat down, his palms clasped together and his elbows resting on the desktop. "Lillian, we will get absolutely nowhere with this if we scream and shout at each other. Where do we go from here?" he spoke with restraint as he looked up at me with his chin resting on his fingertips.

At a complete loss for words, he is, my Chris, I thought as I looked at him.

"Like I said, get tested. Then, once we know the outcome, get the children together and tell them what is going on. The next step will be, Chris, that you go back to Cameroon to look for that woman." I could not bring myself to say her name. The enormity of my situation came over me and I was left breathless, so much so that I had to sit down.

"You will go to Cameroon and look for Sophie's mother. You will go and see that she gets treatment. If you have to pay for it, then you pay for it." I paused and then I added softly, "It is the right thing to do, Chris."

At the first light on Sunday, I left for the hospital. I left Chris a note. He did not try to reach me. I left my mobile phone at home and, when I checked for messages upon my return, there were none from him. There were ten missed calls from my girlfriend, Janice. I bet they were dying to know why I missed our lunch date on Friday. Well, they would have to wait. They would all know the answer soon enough. Sophie sleepily opened those black-brown eyes with the impossibly long lashes and smiled at me weakly when she heard my voice. I spent the better part of Sunday next to her bed, talking to her and reading nursery rhymes. I told her stories of my boys, anecdotes about them from the time when they were little. She had to learn a new language, and she had to get used to me.

Christian, Jr. returned home late on Sunday afternoon. He did not even notice the silence in the house, as he was too involved in playing the latest computer game he'd gotten from his friend.

Monday arrived as a beautiful, glorious sunshine day that broke with a clear sky and many colours. There was birdsong in the air and butterflies in my garden. None of this did anything to change the heaviness of my heart, to lift me out of the blackness of a depression so great it left me breathless. I objectively could feel myself spiralling down into the pit of the darkness but I was helpless to prevent it.

On Monday morning Chris and I dropped Christian at school. He chatted on about this and that and as usual could not wait to get out of the car fast enough at school as his mates were already waiting for him. He did not notice the heavy silence in the car.

We drove straight to the hospital after dropping off our son. Chris did not want to go in at the hospital. He parked the car and rolled down the window on his side. From this action I gathered he would not go in with me. So I said nothing to him as I opened the door and left the car. I would go in alone in that case. We left the hospital grounds in silence. Chris did not ask how Sophie was, and I did not offer any information. The next stop would be our doctor's office.

The receptionist greeted us friendly, she has known us for years. She ushered us straight back to the doctor.

"Morning, Anton." He kissed me on the cheek and shook Chris' hand.

We settled down on the chairs in front of his desk. He took a seat behind the desk. He placed one hand on top of the other on the notepad lying ready on the desk. At first he looked at me and then at Chris, questioningly.

"So what brings the two of you here this morning? You are the picture of excellent health, the both of you?"

I looked at Chris and then at Anton. "We need to be tested for HIV," I said.

He said nothing but just continued looking at the both of us. I could see the questions in his eyes. Anton knew about my involvement with the AIDS orphans.

Chris cleared his throat. "It's me, Anton. I brought this possibility into our relationship."

Anton sat back in his chair. He was a tall, big man, and he had known me ever since I married Chris. He and Chris were at university together. Anton diagnosed my pregnancies, and he was there when I gave birth to each of my boys. He did house calls for sudden fevers in the middle of the night, and I regarded him as a very, very dear friend of the family.

"Do you want to tell me about it?" He looked at Chris.

"I have just found out, actually. It is a very long story," Chris squirmed in his chair. Then he continued "Apparently the woman I had unprotected sex with in Cameroon, well, she has full blown AIDS."

Anton looked from Chris to me, his expression unchanged. "Okay," he said, but the way in which he said it, did not sound okay at all. "This does not mean you are necessarily infected." His gaze was fixed on Chris.

Chris continued, "There is more, Anton. She had a child…that is …she has a child…a little girl. She has AIDS and, in fact, is in hospital right now. Unfortunately the child could be mine, Anton. The timeframe is correct. It corresponds with the age of the child. This means the woman was already infected when we had." He left the sentence open.

I closed it for him, "Sex." Chris and I looked at each other, and Anton looked at the both of us.

The good doctor got up and moved to the trolley with syringes and needles, "Who will go first?"

We drove home in absolute silence. Chris drove much too fast, and I refused to speak up, as I normally would have. At home I got out, ran up the stairs and locked my bedroom door behind me.

The waiting period was the worst. I would drop down in my favourite chair, and the horrid thoughts were upon me like a pack of hyenas. My mind feverishly dissected the past sixteen months. Have I felt sick? Did I have the flu? Have I noticed a painful rash on my skin? Have I suddenly lost weight? Feverishly I tried to remember in the minutest detail the state of my health during the last few months.

Once I could find nothing, absolutely nothing, which might point to a possible infection, I turned my thoughts toward Chris' health. I ran through the same questions and, once again, came up with nothing.

Then my mind started on the "what ifs." *What if our health condition was so excellent an infection would not show until two or three years from now? What if that dreaded virus slowly replicated until, suddenly, after having a cold, it closed in and shut down our immune systems?* In circles, which became ever wider, my mind led me on a wild goose chase because all I could do now was wait for the results.

We were expected back at Anton's rooms the following afternoon at four o'clock. He would discuss the results with us. He said they would do double test to make double sure of the result. As I waited, I drove myself crazy by thinking that I could not possibly have the disease and then again, there is no reason why I should not be infected. I was angry about my very healthy sex life with my husband. In between I cried as I contemplated my future of living with HIV and what changes I would have to make to my lifestyle.

Night eventually fell as I sat there staring out over the land of the Dark Continent. The beauty was totally unobserved by me on this night as my whole life fell apart in front of my very eyes.

Neither Chris nor I felt like eating that night even though we probably should have kept up our strength. Selina just shook her head and cleared the dinner from the table after the fifth ring of the bell. Christian had his meal in front of the television, as there was a sports programme he simply had to watch and, as usual, Selina regarded his every wish as her command.

As I got ready to leave for the hospital that evening, Selina just looked at me and muttered something under her breath. She was so wise, my Selina. She knew. I was sure she knew. In all the years she had been with us, I came to realize she knew everything that happened in our household. She knew what happened in all our relationships within our garden walls. But she would never start a discussion or even ask an inappropriate question. She would wait for me to talk. Inevitably, I would.

Eventually it was Tuesday afternoon. I sat next to Sophie's bed. Her condition remained unchanged despite all my efforts to haul her back from the jaws of death. The anti-retroviral medications and antibiotics the doctors were pumping into her system were not yet showing any effect. Sophie opened her eyes every now and then, only to assure herself I was there, stroking her legs or rubbing her feet. I say this because she seemed to look directly at me, her eyes searching to find me in the room. Then she would vanish again to a place where she had no pain or discomfort.

When the time came, I got up to kiss her little forehead. The eyelids fluttered open and immediately shut again. She sighed before she rolled her head in the opposite direction. It was time to go to Anton to hear the sentence he would pronounce over my life.

Chris' car was already in the car park when I arrived and he was pacing up and down in the waiting room as I entered. *Like a caged animal,* I thought. There was an old lady sitting on a chair, and she looked suspiciously and nervously at him.

He looked at me and smiled but said nothing. I went to him but I could not bring myself to say anything. I stopped in front of him but I could not bring myself to touch him, even to lay my hand on his arm. My hands were sweaty, and I could feel the beginnings of a dull migraine at the back of my left eye.

Slightly after four o'clock, we were ushered into the room. Anton sat behind the desk.

"How are you?" He looked at me but from the way he asked me, he did not really expect an answer. He could imagine what a wreck I was. A slight smile creased the laugh lines at the corners of his eyes. He was a kind man. The kindness and compassion he felt toward humanity emanated from him. If one should receive such dreadful news, then someone like Anton should tell it.

We sat down on the two chairs in front of the desk. As my chair was too close for comfort to Chris', I moved it slightly away. Both men carefully observed this gesture. Anton cleared his throat and then opened a folder on the desk.

"Let's get straight to the point," he said. He looked at the laboratory reports in front of him, first the one page and then the second page. Then he cleared his throat again. The sweat was pouring down my forehead, my hands were clammy, and I felt icy cold even though I could feel my blouse sticking to my skin on my back. I felt like throwing up.

"The results are negative," he said slowly. Then louder, "The results are negative for you that is, Lilly."

"Chris," he paused. He looked up from the paper and into Chris' eyes, "I am sorry, your test came back positive." He had such sadness in his voice. Chris' arms dropped to hang by his side. He had turned a deathly shade of pale.

I jumped out of the chair, grabbed my bag, which stood on the floor by my feet, and ran from the room, leaving the door wide open. I did not even wait for Anton to continue, to speak of the many ways by which this disease could be managed. I just ran.

I ran past all the patients waiting in the waiting room, and I did not care that they all stared at me. I had completely lost my control and my composure. I ran outside and as soon as I was in the car park, I threw up. There was nothing in my stomach but the contractions kept on coming and through it all, I cried loud sobs like a child. My head felt like exploding, my whole body hurt from the powerful contractions, and I howled on the sidewalk of the car park in front of Anton's consultation rooms.

I was not HIV positive and I would not get AIDS. This refrain ran through my mind over and over again on my way home. My beautiful, beloved husband was infected. I drove like a maniac, screeching around the street corners and jumping red traffic lights as far as was possible during peak traffic hour on this Tuesday afternoon.

III.

At home I ran up the stairs to my room two stairs at a time. I could barely wait to get under the shower. The hot water coursing over me made me feel as though I could wash away the anguish and anxiety of the past couple of days. I felt as though I had aged many years since Friday morning, and my body was aching. I screamed under the shower and the tears flowed unchecked over my cheeks, mixing with the hot water and running away at my feet, flowing away from me and taking my pain with it. What could I have done in my life to deserve this? How could I continue to live with a husband who was carrying that deathly virus inside of him? I prayed like never before to the merciful God to please give me answers!

I put on my cozy, white robe and sheepskin slippers. I felt cold despite the pleasant spring weather. I descended the staircase in search of Selina or Christian, someone to talk to.

I found Chris in his study. We did not speak. I looked at him, and I felt sorry for him. He had also been to hell and back, and the traces were etched on his face. He stood by the window, and he looked at me.

I walked across and straight into his arms. It was the first contact we had since this nightmare began. I realized how much I had missed his closeness, and I was slightly awed by my need to be hugged and held by him. I have missed my husband. I felt so deeply sorry for him. I have loved this man for the longest time.

After what seemed to have been an eternity, I pulled away. I looked up at him and he bent down toward me. His lips touched mine with the softest, featheriest of kisses. Caressing slowly, lightly, his lips brushed across my lips. I could taste his breath. His hands moving up and down my back and squeezing my buttocks. I could feel the passion soaring between us and I pulled away.

"Chris," I put some distance between us and I tightened the belt of my robe at the front again. "Chris," I said again, "we have to talk this over. This thing that happened sixteen months ago."

"What do you want to know, Lilly? What else can I possibly say to all this which have happened the past few days? You know

49

this story better than me," he added sardonically and moved to sit down on one of the couches. "You can say I got what was due to me. I have the virus and you don't."

"Chris, you simply cannot shrug this off like that. You are the father of my children. You are my husband for God's sake! We have been married for more than twenty years! We need to face this together. I will not and I cannot abandon you." I shuddered and I rubbed my upper arms. No solution came to my mind.

"What do you want, Lilly? I will tell you all you want to know," he said it like I had asked him what we were having for dinner, casual, matter-of-fact.

"Start at the beginning. Start with how you came to meet... Sophie's mother." I sat down opposite him with my feet tucked beneath me and a big cushion on my lap. I needed something to keep my hands occupied.

Chris got up and walked over to the liquor cabinet to pour himself a very stiff whisky. Neat. No rocks. He took a big gulp, then a slower sip to savour. It was as though he drew strength from the liquid in the glass. He came back to where I was sitting and took a seat opposite me.

He looked at me intensely, then put one arm on the backrest and the other on the side of the couch, holding the glass. Legs relaxed, stretched out in front of him, he leaned his head back and closed his eyes. Softly he began to speak.

"A little over two years ago I had to go on a routine visit to Cameroon to get updated on the projects we have up there." He paused, then continued." This time around, a young woman accompanied the company driver who came to pick me up at the airport. Not the regular elderly lady, but a tiny young thing with a beautiful laugh. Whenever she laughed it made you want to laugh along with her. She seemed to be lots of fun." He paused, took a sip of his drink. "Lilly, are you sure you want to hear this?"

I was stunned about what he was telling me. I was hearing about a side of my husband, of more than twenty years, I did not know existed before today. Could he have been attracted to someone who appeared so frivolous, so lightheaded?

"Go on," I said. My mouth was so dry my tongue stuck to the insides of my cheeks as I spoke.

"She was young and stared at me with these huge adoring eyes. She wanted to know everything about my life. Everything. She wanted to know if I was married, if I had children, how long had I been with the company, all questions I would normally regard as rude and intruding, but this is Darkest Africa. Up there on the continent there is a different pulse. A different heartbeat. People don't react or act as they would do down here. Or in Europe. Or in civilisation elsewhere. Things are just different up there."

He took another swig. He had so often in the past asked me to accompany him on his trips into Africa. I always declined. I always had things to do down here. The children needed me. I had a function at which I absolutely had to be present or a charity meeting at which most important decisions had to be made—fundraisers which absolutely would not have been a success if I was not present. Too busy to live my very-near-perfect life and being Lillian Johnston, had I forgotten to look at my husband with wonder in my eyes? Had I forgotten to make him feel important? To hang on his every word?

He continued, "So we drove back to the office. She was chattering away and filling me in on my schedule for the next two days. She said she was the new executive assistant in the office. She was so proud to hold this position as her family was extremely poor. She offered to show me around Douala if I felt up to it and, as I had nothing planned after work that evening, I said yes. I did not feel like staying in my hotel room all alone or going to dine in solitude. I have had enough of that on my solitary trips abroad."

He looked at me for the longest time before he continued again. I just sat there, hardly breathing. Too scared to say anything in case I burst into tears. I did not want to risk stopping him now.

"So she came to collect me from the hotel that evening. Happy and gay and just being a friendly young lady out to offer a gentleman company during the evening meal. We went to a bistro in the waterfront area on the Wouri River. It is most charming there, and one can really still feel the French influence. A strange mixture of the familiarity of the African mixed with a certain French flair.

"After we dined, we decided to walk back to the hotel. It was not far to go but very pretty all along the river. Then it happened. No romance, no courting—just mating.

Natural. Inevitable. We simply came together. We did not exchange niceties. There were no words. I cannot tell you why, and I cannot tell you what. All I can say is that we had sex. Brief and explosive and then it was over. In the darkness, against some wall next to the Wouri River. We continued in silence to my hotel. In front of the hotel, she got into a taxi and I never saw her again. She was not at the office the next day, at least, I did not see her. I never heard from her again. Until Friday."

By now the tears were streaming down my face. When would I stop crying? It seemed as though I had done nothing but cry the last couple of days. "Chris, how many Ayandas have there been in your life? How many more will come to our gate with a baby on the arm? By your thoughtless act of fornication—one cannot even call it intimacy—you have brought potential death into our partnership." My voice broke.

He was on his feet and enfolded me in his arms. He showered kisses on my forehead and on my hair. "Sweetheart, my angel, my darling, please, please forgive me. There is no one else. She was the only one. I cannot tell you what happened except to say I was stupid and careless and idiotic. I love you, Lilly. Only you. You must believe me."

I hung on to him for dear life. I just could not let him go. We shared a quarter of a century together. Could I forgive him and move on from this day forward without ever referring to this episode again?

But I could not move on from this day. Chris has tested positive. Nothing will ever be the same again.

We just sat like that on the couch. Hanging on to each other. Not talking. Chris held me till my crying stopped. I kept my face buried in his chest so I was not sure if I heard him sobbing or if it was my imagination. I did not lift my head to check. I could not be strong for anyone right now.

Christian poked his head round the door after the longest time of us sitting like this. He started to speak but when he noticed how Chris was cradling me and I was crying, he rolled his eyes and left the study, closing the door behind him. I guess whatever he needed, Gogo would help him with.

We did not go to have dinner. We simply went to bed. In silence. Slowly getting undressed and getting into bed, each one on his side of the huge king-size bed. I immediately turned on my side away from Chris. He did the same. We were both so very tired we fell asleep immediately.

Shortly after midnight on Tuesday, my mobile phone rang. Chris switched on his bedside lamp as I fumbled for the phone next to my bed. It was the hospital. Sophie had taken a turn for the worst.

We dressed in a hurry. Jeans and a sweater, the night was characteristically cold, typical for this time of year here in the Highveld. We sped through the empty streets toward the hospital. This time it was Chris at the wheel.

We both hurried together down the corridors toward the paediatric intensive care unit. I greeted the staff and introduced Chris. "He is Sophie's father." The bewildered expressions said it all but there was no time to lose.

We stood next to her bed. Her little fingers curled around my index finger as I stroked her little legs. She opened her eyes for a long time, staring at me. Only at me. She never once turned her head to look at Chris. Then she smiled at me for the longest time, closed her eyes, and her head rolled to the side. She did not open her eyes again. She was gone. To the land of the angels, a little person who had to pay the price for the carelessness of two grownups, adults who were supposed to have known better.

I stared across at Chris long after the nurse had come to place the sheet over Sophie. He said nothing. He simply stood there staring at the shape beneath the white sheet. The only sign of emotion was the clenching of his jaws. His arms hanging by his sides and his head bent. We drove home in complete silence, each one busy with his or her own thoughts.

I organized the funeral. It was the priest, Chris, and I who attended. The tombstone was an angel carved out of white marble and simply engraved Sophie Johnston. Her father and her family acknowledged her as part of their family, and it was there for all the world to see. I planted a rosebush on her grave. One which bore white roses to symbolize her innocence.

IV.

It was a beautiful day on the Highveld. For those who know, the days are always beautiful here on the Highveld. In winter, it can be bitterly cold but the sun mostly shines, and the sky is blue. During the winter, the surrounding grasslands are set alight. Then there's an acrid smell in the air, sometimes the smoke from this burning grassland gets so intense one can taste it. Then, after the first rains, new grass grows back prolific again, the landscape turns green and there are running streams after every thunderstorm, which normally comes in the afternoons.

It was almost noon. I was still wearing my gown and slippers. My hair was unwashed, and I had dark rings under my eyes. I stood in front of my window looking out over the garden. Phineas was weeding under the large acorn tree by the barbeque area. He was sitting in the shade and leaning back against the trunk every now and then. As usual he was drawing lazily on his pipe, just enough to keep the tobacco smouldering and, therefore, keep the insects at bay.

Somewhere in the house I could hear Selina vacuuming.

The day was so normal I almost forgot the absolute anguish and turmoil inside of me. The sheer horror of the past week, or was it already ten days? God! How was it possible that all of this had happened within such a short period of time? This horrendous maelstrom inside of me, I had done absolutely nothing to deserve this tearing apart of my...our lives...how could this be?

I hugged myself as I sank into my chair by the window. I had no idea where Chris was. He slept in this room only once since this catastrophe turned our world upside down. At some point he must have come in to remove his clothes. Come to think of it, I had not seen much of him during the past two days. I have been holed up here in my room.

Chris, Jr. popped in early this morning and all he had to say was "Jeez Mom, you look terrible! Mom, I am going to Mark this afternoon and his mom will drop me off later." He kissed me on the forehead and was gone before I had time to answer him or say anything regarding his plans for the day.

My boys....We will need to tell them about this mess. Soon it will be the school spring break and they will all be home for the holidays. We will have to tell them that their father has—oh dear, God, no!

I had a queasy feeling in my stomach and I felt like throwing up. Chris had tested positive for THAT virus. What implication did this have for me, for us? I saw all these brave people who wore T-shirts stating that they were HIV- positive, so many prominent persons here in this country had died of AIDS, famous people sympathized and held concerts and even I took care of babies who had that god-awful virus, but my own husband?

To sympathize and sing for the cause, it was a totally different story if this virus personally affected one…if one's life was falling apart because of it. The virus was pulsating and alive under my own roof even as I spoke! How could I deal with this fact? What would our friends say? Would they stand by us, support us? How could I inform them? Should I organize a dinner party, dress up in fancy gear and when the band takes a break after the main course I announce to them that Chris has the virus as well? Sort of like a coming-out-party? Oh God! The questions! They would want to know how he became infected? Should I say blood transfusion? I could not say he shared a needle with a drug addict as everyone who knew him knew how vehemently he despised drugs and the entire milieu connected with addicts.

As I was sitting there in that chair, drowning in this pit of self-pity, sorrow and sadness, my mobile phone rang on the bedside table. The same happy, catchy tone, which always made me happy and now sounded so perfectly out of place. So I slowly got up to go and answer it. I noticed the pain in my body and I moved slowly.

"Hallo," I almost got a fright at the sound of my own listless voice.

"Lilly? Is that you?" I heard the voice of my dearest friend Janice on the other end of the line.

"Hi Jan—" I could not continue because I simply burst into tears.

"Are you at home, Lilly?" she asked.

"Yes," I managed to stammer.

"Stay where you are, I will be right there" she said and then she hung up the phone on me before I could say anything further.

I just fell over on my bed and buried my face in the thick welcoming folds of my goose down duvet.

When would this uncontrollable crying ever stop? I have never cried this much during the past thirty years as I had during those last ten days!

Janice was my closest friend. We immediately took a liking to each other all those many years ago when our eldest sons started school together.

We sat in the same row on that morning so many years ago. Connor sat next to me. Very proud in his brand new school uniform. Shoes polished and shiny, socks pulled up properly and his tie perfectly knotted – Chris did it that morning and showed him how a gentleman knotted a tie. As Connor is the eldest, the other two boys stood by and watched attentively because they strived to be just like Connor – their big brother and the leader of the pack. Christopher and Christian, Jr. saw Connor as the role model in their lives. The hero of the three boys was undoubtedly their father and then came Connor. He could climb a tree like no other, he could catch a rain spider (and believe me those are the scariest creatures alive with their massive hairy bodies and long legs and on top of this they could jump really far) and he could outrun Mommy! These were reasons enough to idolize Connor.

So there we sat in the big hall of this very old boys' preparatory school with pictures of old boys on the walls, boys who grew up to become men who were leading personalities in our society in those days and of those who had past on but during their prime, played roles in establishing the economy of our country, role models to the young ones who now sat there in those pews and would come to revere the names of these "Old Boys" in due course during their time inside those hallowed halls.

Chris sat at the aisle, I sat next to him, close to me (but not too close because the guys might just think that he was scared) sat Connor, then Chris, Jr. (because he was the youngest and had to be protected by his two older brothers) and then finally Christopher at the end of our line.

I was both sad and proud, sad because I had to let Connor go—every mother feels like this when her eldest child starts school – and proud because of the young man whom I have brought here today. My boy Connor. I was sure that every mother reflected on all the hours invested in her child on such a momentous occasion such as the first day of school…all the hours of love, of teaching, of storytelling and play and of simply being happy and blessed to have them in your life.

As I sat there, deep in thought and reflection, another family entered the row of seats where we sat. I turned my head to look left and looked straight into Janice's eyes. I liked her on sight. Her bright smile lit up her face immediately as she leaned over to shake my hand and introduce herself.

"Hi, I'm Jan and this is my son Jonathan. He is a first timer today."

I took her hand "Hi, I'm Lilly and my son Connor here is also a first timer."

The boys eyed one another—instantly summarizing each other—and because he was raised to be a gentleman, Connor got up and shook Jonathan's hand.

The boys became inseparable from that day on. We often joked that we should rename Connor to David because of the bond they shared. Jonathan became like a son in our house and Connor in Janice's house.

Janice came from Cape Town—Constantia to be exact. She had four sisters and a big brother and through her I came to know how wonderful it was to have a big family. Christmases were spent with all the aunties, uncles and cousins on the family's wine estate, there was always support during difficult times and always a birthday to remember of someone in the family.

I envied Jan because of her family—not envy in a horrible, negative way, but in an amazed and admiring way. It made me realize how much I missed having my own family in the way of parents and siblings and what could have been had it not been for that crash which killed my parents all those years ago.

Jan was married to Peter. A very clever man with an incredibly dry sense of humour. He worked as the chief financial officer for a large international company and was also often traveling.

They had a wonderful marriage – for all one can ascertain when looking in from the outside.

Besides Jonathan, they had two daughters. Twin girls who looked so much alike that even Peter had to look twice to tell them apart. Lucy and Gemma with the long, curly blonde hair and the baby blue eyes. They looked perfectly angelic but they were the greatest tomboys a person could meet – my boys adored them and regarded them as their own sisters. Jonathan had red hair and freckles with the same blue eyes as his mother.

My friend had beautiful blue eyes with laugh lines and long blonde hair which she wore twisted into a French roll at the back of her head. When she left it loose, it cascaded down her back to below her shoulder blades. As she wore it in this twisted roll at the back, she always looked effortlessly elegant.

When I looked into her eyes that morning at the school so many years ago now, I felt as if I knew her already since a very long time. We spoke often – daily, I would say – and we saw each other at least twice per week and we never ran out of topics to talk about.

Except during these last two weeks. I have not spoken to or seen Janice. This never happened if we were both in town.

And this is how she found me half an hour later in my pajamas, hair undone and dirty, eyes almost swollen shut from all the crying and dreadfully pale.

The knock on the door was soft and before I had time to answer it, the door swung open and Janice stood there.

She took one look at me, then turned around and closed the door.

"Dear God, Lilly! What happened to you?" she said once the door was shut. She took me in her arms and I clung to her, dry sobs wracking my body.

For the longest time we just sat like that. Janice holding me and rocking me gently from side to side. Like I was a baby. Until the sobs subsided and we just sat like this, with me clinging to her. Needing to draw on her strength.

She pulled away to look at me, her hand cradling my cheek. There was great concern and worry in her eyes.

"Lilly, you need to tell me what happened." She held me at arm's length. Then she continued " but first, I am going to run you a lovely bath, then you are going to eat something and then we are going to talk." With these words she got up, pulled me up and supported me with her arm around my waist whilst walking with me to the bathroom en-suite.

She undressed me and helped me to lower myself into the fragrant water. Then she left to go down to the kitchen in order to get something to eat.

I lay there, soaking in my big tub filled with lavender fragranced water and tried to empty my mind. "I am so, so tired" I thought. I felt like I was falling and I imagined that the base jumpers must feel like this—or maybe they don't and I just imagined that they do. Freefalling out of the sky with no string to pull in order to open a parachute, or knowing that there is no net below me to catch me. Just falling, speeding toward rock solid bottom with an incredible velocity and I did not know how to stop. I was indeed unable to stop.

I was drawn back to the present by Jan's voice.

She was talking from my bedroom.

"Hmmmm, this smells so good!" She called. I could hear her placing a tray on the glass tabletop in my bedroom next door.

The next moment her head appeared around the corner of the door.

"Do you feel like coming out or do you want to eat in the bath?" she asked.

I turned my head to look at her, "I'll come out in a minute."

I sank below the water, submerging myself for a few seconds.

"This does feel good," I thought to myself. Then I got out and wrapped myself in a large fluffy bath sheet with a smaller one wrapped around my wet hair.

Janice had made herself very comfortable in one of the wing-backs in front of the bay window. She opened the windows and the faintly sweet smelling spring air was drifting into the room.

On the table were a tray with a most delicious turkey salad sandwich and a jug of homemade ice tea.

"Make yourself comfortable, Lil. This is all yours." She looked at me and I saw the kindness and worry in her eyes.

Silence. We were so comfortable with each other that it did not disturb us to just sit like this, quietly. She knew that I would start to talk when I was good and ready. I knew that she was there for me—always has been—but then again, I never had to tell her—or anyone else for that matter—what I was about to tell Jan now.

I finished my sandwich and drank down half a glass of ice tea in one go – not very ladylike, I must admit – but I did not realize how hungry and thirsty I had been.

"Chris has AIDS," I said it softly.

She looked over at me as though she did not hear me. Her face was blank. Then, as my words sank in.

"I beg your pardon, Lilly, what did you just say?" Janice dropped her arms so that they hung limply at the side of the chair.

I cleared my throat. Placed the glass back on the table. Stared at my hands as though to find the answer there.

I looked up and met her stare. "What I mean to say is Chris has been infected with HIV."

The next minute she was next to my chair on her knees, holding both my hands. "Oh my God, Lilly!" Her eyes filled with tears. "Oh my God, how absolutely dreadful for you!" She hugged me close and I could feel the sobs wracking her body this time. I just sat there. I had no more tears left. I just sat there holding on to my dearest friend who was crying because she shared my pain.

After a long while, the tears subsided and she looked up at me.

"This obviously is a very long story, Lilly. Start at the beginning." And so I started at the beginning, with many pauses and breaks in between because we both cried when I came to tell about Sophie. Janice sat there, on the plush carpet by my feet, never letting go of my hands, wiping away my tears and wiping away her own and offering me tea to drink when my voice broke and my throat became too dry to speak from all the emotion.

The phone rang many times during my monologue. Gogo must have answered. Chris Jr. must have come home because it was late afternoon when I finally stopped speaking. Outside, the spectacle of dusk had started and still Jan and I just sat there. In the silence, finally.

Eventually she got up and phoned Pete. All she said was "Hon, I am at Lilly's. I will be a while. You guys go ahead with dinner. We will talk when I get home." This was how uncomplicated their relationship was. It always amazed me how easy they could be with each other.

V.

Hi, I am Janice. Here I stand in the bedroom of my dearest friend, Lilly. The sanctuary she shared with her husband, the domain which belongs to two people who share their lives. The place where they love and live and plot the direction their lives will go, together, as a family.

I have just heard the most horrendous news a person could wish to hear…my darling Lilly's husband has been infected. She is crushed—absolutely totally destroyed.

And yet should I go ahead and tell her or do I keep quiet and then forever keep silent about what else I know? Will it be fair toward her if I keep quiet or will it be in her best interest to know what I know? We are supposed to be best friends – I love her as though she is my sister and yet. How would I feel if she knew what I know and she did not tell me? Would I forgive her? Would I feel betrayed if she knew this terrible thing and did not tell me? Dare I tell her and thus come between her and her husband?

I decided to go with my first feeling and tell her.

"Lilly" I could not continue because my heart beat at the top of my throat and I could not breathe.

She looked at me with those sad eyes. Dull and full of pain.

"Lilly, I have something to tell you." I started again. I moved the wingback chair closer to her and sat down. I leaned across and took her hands in mine. I looked her in the eyes and continued softly.

"Lilly, I don't know how to tell you this but I figured if I said nothing you will be more mad at me than if I said it so. Chris has been cheating on you for years." I held on to her hands as she stared at me and I waited for this knowledge to sink in.

"No, no," she groaned, pulled her hands out of mine and locked them around her drawn up knees.

For the longest time she did not say anything. I sat there waiting for her to speak. She squirmed in the chair and she moaned like a wounded animal.

Eventually she lifted her eyes to mine. "For how long have you known, Janice?"

"For the longest time, Lilly. I could not tell you."

"Why, Janice? Why did you not tell me? Why did you wait until it is too late? I could also have been infected? Why did you not warn me earlier?" Lilly got up from her chair. Like an old person who had no strength left, she lifted herself up and then stood next to the chair for the longest time, her hand resting on the chair for support.

I simply sat there, letting her hurt wash over me. Prepared to deal with it as she was not strong enough to carry this load alone. I would have reacted the same way. In fact, I would have ranted and raved.... but Lilly had almost no more strength left. She looked beaten and incredibly sad.

"Lilly, if I told you he was messing around two years ago would you have believed me? If I told you this five years ago would you have believed me? Would it have been any easier? Yes, I blame myself because I kept quiet but you are my friend! I did not want to say anything to jeopardize our friendship. If I said something before today, you would have taken Chris' side and I would have lost you. I need for you to know that I am there for you, my family and Pete, we will always be there for you and the boys. Pete has known for longer than me. Why do you think he never became a friend of Chris'? Chris knew that Pete knew about his whoring around."

"Whoring around?" Lilly asked, "What do you mean, Jan? If you say he was whoring around then there must have been more than one? Who were they?" Lilly fixed me with her eyes and I looked down at my hands.

For the longest time I could not bring myself to answer her or to look up."Yes, Lilly, there was more than one. I don't know how many but I know of three…" my voice trailed off as I looked up and saw her dropping her head in her hands.

"Do I know them, Jan?" her voice was soft, defeated.

"I don't know, Lilly. It does not matter if you know them or not. The fact is that he has been unfaithful to you for a long, long time and I thank God that you did not get any disease from him and that it is eventually out in the open."

We just sat like this. After a long time of silence, Lilly got up. She looked at me and she smiled. A sad, lopsided smile. Her skin was dreadfully pale and I only now noticed that she had bags under her eyes with dark rings. The face of a woman who had gone through absolute torment, misery and sadness over the past couple of weeks. She came to where I sat. She took my hands in hers. "How can I ever thank you for what you have done for me today? The fact that you were here with me and what you have told me, have helped me come to some conclusions about my life. There are some decisions which I have to take. I cannot go on like this."

She closed her eyes for a moment, a tear rolling out from the corner of her right eye. For a moment she stood like this, then she breathed deeply and said "I will be all right. You need to go home to your family now. I will call you tomorrow."

With this, I got up, realizing that she needed to digest all of this. I did not speak anymore, just gave her a hug and then I left. At the door I turned back to blow her a kiss and then I closed the door behind me without looking back.

With tears streaming down my cheeks, I let myself out the front door. I did not encounter anything or anyone on my way out. As I approached the gates, it opened silently. Lilly must have stood there in her bedroom watching me leave.

VI.

Janice just left. I sighed as I sank back into the chair.

I could not cry anymore. I had no more tears left. Inside of me it felt as though a living creature was eating away. I had no emotion left, the only thing I knew for sure was I loved my sons, and I had to survive in order to be there for them. I could no longer hide. I was a mother, protector of the home, and I had done nothing wrong. I had to decide what to do about this marriage.

First things first: I got up. I got dressed. I put on makeup and pushed my hair back with an elegant hairband. I put on stockings and high heels as though I were going out for a night on the town. Then I went downstairs in search of the father of my children.

That's right, no more "my husband." The fact was that he was still the father of my children. He chose to forfeit being my husband. As his car was in the driveway, I assumed he had to be home, and the most likely place for him to be was his study. So I went there first and bingo! There he was. Sitting in the chair behind the desk, talking on his mobile. The moment he saw me standing in the door, he broke off his conversation and put the phone on the desk.

"Good evening, Chris." I sounded almost cheerful. I surprised myself with my acting ability. In reality, I felt like throwing his phone against the wall. I must have entered the room very quietly if he did not even hear me approach.

"Who was that on the phone?" I have never, in all our married life, asked such a question, as I always assumed it was a business call if he did not volunteer the information.

He looked bewildered. "No one you would know, Lilly," he answered.

"No, I bet I wouldn't, would I now, Chris?" I answered back, with a slight smile around the corners of my mouth. "Are you trying to warn them now that you know about your status?"

Chris looked completely ashen. "What do you mean, darling?"

I smiled. Ice cold. The smile never reaching my eyes.

I looked him square in the eyes, "You have messed with the wrong person, Chris. I almost feel sorry for you."

Then I turned toward the door and said "Good heavens, I am starving. Have you eaten already? Where is Chris, Jr.?" And with these words, I walked out the door in search of my son.

I was functioning normally. At least in my mind, considering the circumstances, I was functioning normally. Then again, who determined the parameters for normal behaviour? If one compared me to the person who fluttered around town one month ago, then I was definitely not normal. So, were we ever normal in the eyes of the beholder? I once determined the normalcy of people. In fact, I was always quick to point out when something was not normal according to my judgment and my standards.

Presently, I stood at the airport, waiting for my eldest son to arrive from London. By the end of that day, I would have had all three of my sons under my roof. Like we said in Africa: I would be able to cover them all under the same blanket once again.

It was a great sadness that I would have to tell them all of what had happened over the past couple of weeks. After long and hard soul searching, I had decided to tell them everything. The boys were not babies anymore. They knew the facts of life. Chris had been impossible to talk with. I did not know where he had disappeared to, but he'd left. He vanished straight after I left his study two nights ago, and no one in the house had heard from him or seen him since. I expected him home tonight, as he knew the boys would all be there.

I began to contemplate what it would be like to have my sons home under the current circumstances, when I saw Connor. Good heavens, how he had changed since I saw him three months ago! He had grown into a gorgeous young man. He had gained a certain substance to his frame, the jaw being angular now with slight stubble showing through. The heavy fringe falling over the left eye. I remember how, as a boy, we always teased him because of his long eyelashes. He positively had the girls drooling while he was still at school, and I'd really rather not know how they carried on once he was away at university and a man and all. In any event, in my eyes he was still my boy and always would be, no matter how old he grew to be.

He spotted me standing at the back of the crowd and came striding toward me, a wide grin breaking over his features. I moved forward into his arms.

"Mom, it is so great to see you." We clung to each other for a moment and then I looked up into his face.

"You too, sweetheart. I missed you, big guy." I looked at the single bag he had standing on the floor next to him. "Is this all the luggage you have?"

"Yip, I still have lots of clothes at home here, Mom. Have you forgotten? Besides, I don't need much. If my memory serves me well, Gogo keeps the washing machine going around the clock. Speaking of her, how is she? How is Dad? Where is he, by the way?"

"Slow down, dearest, catch your breath. Everybody is just fine. I think Dad is at the office. At least, that is where he is supposed to be." I tried to speak as normal as possible but Connor noticed the slight insecurity in my voice.

"What do you mean 'supposed' to be? He said he would be here for the holidays, Mom. Where else would he be?" Connor looked at me askance, and I quickly put my large sunglasses back on.

"Of course, darling. Just pulling your leg. Come on, let's get you home and unpacked." I put my arm around him as we walked off toward the parking garage.

Along the way we spoke of everything, the things which made life normal, like what time Christopher would arrive home this afternoon, the sports events, all the new roads being built around Johannesburg, politics, how his friends were doing who stayed on here in South Africa in order to go to university. General chitchat. Before we realized it, we were driving up the driveway toward our house.

Phineas came up to the car to shake Connor's hand. Phineas used to push the boys around the garden in the wheelbarrow when they were just naughty little boys. He told them endless stories of the African bush and contributed greatly to Connor's love of storytelling.

"*Umfaan*, how are you? Eish, you got big now, bru! You gotta many galfriends now!" Phineas laughed his raspy laugh and promptly broke into a cough because of all the smoking.

"Hey, Phineas, my man! How are you? You should stop smoking that poison! Its much healthier to chase away the flies than to smoke them away!" Connor placed his arm around Phineas' bony shoulders.

At this, Phineas broke into a gale of laughter, which ended with him coughing until he could not breathe any more.

I stood to the side observing the scene, thinking how great it was for the children in my family to have grown up in a milieu where there were people who accompanied them through their lives into adulthood. People who helped contribute to the wonderful persons my sons had become.

As I turned around to walk toward the house, I saw the gates opening and Chris' car coming toward us.

I kept going but Connor went to say hello to his father. I left them alone and went into the house toward the kitchen. Tonight the most important people in my life would be at my dinner table and I have planned to prepare for each one, his special dish.

Dinner was fabulous. For a few hours I completely forgot about the turmoil in my life as I listened to the boys talking. Every now and then I could feel Chris' eyes on me but I pretended not to notice and looked at my sons instead.

After dinner I went outside. Alone. I was sitting on my terrace with a glass of wine, Chet Baker's latest musical contribution softly playing in the background. All along the driveway torches filled with citronella oil burned. This kept the mosquitoes at bay. Next to me on the table, a gardenia-scented candle burned inside a large mosaic glass holder I had bought on a trip to Morocco. The air was filled with the scent of jasmine and petunias, and I felt safe and happy. This was, after all, the kingdom I created. The boys and their father were in the den, playing a round of snooker and talking men's talk. Even Chris, Jr. was with them and was as usual, drinking in every single moment. These moments will sustain him once everyone has left to go back to where they lived. Then Chris, Jr. would regale his friends with tales about "My brother Connor said ..." and "My brother Christopher said..." and these anecdotes would be told and retold to his friends as though they were gospel. Cast in stone, because his big brothers had said so.

I just sat there, lost in my own thoughts, which were not going anywhere except around in circles—starting at a point only to end at that same point. Somehow I was unable to think outside of these tormenting circles, and, quite frankly, I simply did not want to confront myself by introducing any new pattern of thought. I knew I had to at some point, but not tonight. I needed this reprieve. The night was so beautiful. I revelled in the happiness of having come so far, surviving the onslaught on my sanity, and of having my children with me.

Tomorrow was far away and tomorrow I would tell the children. I did not know how, but somehow I would have to. The two big boys were bound to notice something was wrong.

I woke up early as usual. The birds were singing outside and the sky was just beginning to change colour. Normally, I loved this time alone. I would put on my robe and go down to the kitchen, make a nice hot cup of caffé latté, and sit in the winter garden by the kitchen, watching the world come alive.

I pushed back the covers and swung my legs over the side of the bed. My room was quiet and, as had become the pattern, I had been sleeping alone. Chris must have either left last night or he was sleeping in the guestroom. To be honest, I did not really care.

The scene, which met me in the kitchen, was not quite what I had expected. Chris, Connor, and Christopher were all three sitting at the table in the winter garden. The television was turned off and each had a steaming mug of coffee. On the table in front of them was a tin with rusks. Homemade, might I add. All three were only clad in their boxer shorts. At first I hesitated to step into the room but then I thought better of it and went in.

"Good morning! How come you are all up so early?" I sounded cheerful. I was met by silence. Chris kept looking straight ahead out at the garden. Connor and Christopher looked at me. Then they got up, came over to me, and hugged me. Christopher looked at me for the longest time, turned, and left the room. Connor kept his arm around my shoulders and led me to the table.

"Can I make you your coffee, Mom?" He looked at me.

"What a lovely thought, darling. Yes, please." I sat down in the chair opposite Chris. "Same as always."

"Good morning, Lilly." Chris had the morning voice.

We did not speak to each other, simply waited for Connor to return with my coffee with an uncomfortable silence hanging between us. There was so much to be said. Yet, we had nothing to say.

Connor came back, put the mug with steaming caffé latté down in front of me and sat down.

"Mom, what is going on?" Silence. "I noticed you and Dad did not speak to each other at all last night. Last night we all walked up together after you had gone to bed, and Dad continued down the passage with us in the direction of the guest room. In all my life, you and Dad never slept apart except if he was traveling."

Connor looked at me questioningly. This was a new experience for me, that my son, who was just a little boy not so long ago, could suddenly be the mediator in my marriage! Could this be? Was there not something wrong with this picture? Should children mediate between their own parents?

"Connor, it is a long story. Maybe your father should start—"

He cut me off, "No, Mom, Christopher and I asked him what was going on and he said we should ask you? So, what gives, Mother?" he looked at me questioningly.

"Your father has," I breathed deeply, "had a child by another woman." There, I said it.

Connor looked at me as though he could not quite understand what I was saying. Then he looked at Chris. "What is she saying, Dad? Is it true?"

Chris dropped his face in his hands and for the longest time he remained like that.

Then he rubbed his fingers over his eyes. "Yes," he said softly, "yes, son, I'm afraid your mother is right."

"So where is this child now?" Connor looked from Chris directly to me.

After the longest time, I answered, "She died."

"Fuck," Connor said the word slowly and with such expression in his voice that I looked up at him, shocked. Normally I would scold him for using such base language but, considering the information he was just delivered, I kept quiet.

Connor got up and left.

Chris looked at me and then he spoke. "Lilly, I don't know how to reach you. I want to speak with you but you have locked me out—"

I cut him short. "Speaking of locking someone out, Chris. This what has happened, this tragedy, was merely the tragic tip of the iceberg, wasn't it? I found out accidentally. You would never have had the guts to tell me about what happened if you found out

73

about Sophie before I did, would you, Chris?" I looked at him with fire in my eyes, my voice devoid of warmth.

"Lilly, if you would just let me explain." He looked at me with those beautiful eyes. I felt revulsion and pity. A grownup man who had such potential—such a brilliant mind and intelligence—yet, I pitied him. He was so very poor inside, playing people—me included—for such fools. A master manipulator, one look from him with those eyes would have had me eating out of his hand in the past. Today I felt nothing but absolute repulsion.

"Lilly, the children can hear you. Let us go to the study to talk." He pushed his chair back. Even now, when I was supposed to hate him, I could not help but admire his body. He really kept it in good shape over the years. He still had a six-pack belly even though it now bore the evidence of good living combined with middle age on it. He made a delectable view from the back as well. *Dear God, I was hurting so much inside and still I ached for him. Why did my heart betray me so?*

"Yes, let us go to the study by all means. It won't stay a secret anyway, as I think the boys have a right to know what you have been up to behind all our backs." I took my mug and followed him out the door toward the study.

He walked ahead of me, opened the door, and stood aside in order for me to enter into the room ahead of him, and then he firmly closed the door behind him. I went over to my favourite place on the sofa, settled down comfortably and looked at him. He came to sit down opposite me but he did not reach for my hands across the coffee table.

"Lilly," He said my name softly. He looked at me for the longest time. I kept quiet. At first I looked into his eyes for what felt like an eternity but then I looked down. I was so afraid I would lose my cool and drop my false façade of utter control.

"We really had good times, you and I. Do you remember?"

I cut him short before he could continue, "Yes, Chris, we did have good times."

He continued without missing a beat "I don't want to give that up, Lilly. I cannot bear losing my family. These past couple of weeks…I have done a lot of thinking and I simply cannot and will not give all this up. Without you, the boys…I just can't be without you. I just cannot live without you."

This was too much for me. I jumped up and paced over to his desk with my back toward him. Placed my hands palms down on the cool solid wood surface, closed my eyes and tried to collect myself so that I could speak in a calm manner and not scream at him.

I turned around and crossed my arms over my chest, crossed my legs at the ankles, leaning against the desk, looking at him. I felt like kissing and making love with him, and, at the same time, I wanted to cause him physical pain, I wanted him to feel what I had felt those past weeks, the rawness inside of me. The feeling as if I were standing on a precipice, losing my balance, holding on to my sanity and my life with only a few fingers in order not to finally fall completely into an abyss of pain and loss. I needed to know that he also felt this same emptiness inside, to have a pain that sometimes, in the middle of the night, felt like it was a real entity. That it was lying next to me in bed, and it had me firmly in its grip. The pain that woke me up in the night, ensnared in my bed sheets from all the tossing around—the nightmares were always the same: I saw Chris in the arms of the other women, doing to them what he and I used to do together, causing me to toss and turn and cry out his name, reaching out for him, only to wake up with tears streaming down my cheeks, sobbing and crying. I had even started doubting my own sanity. I thought I would lose it altogether, that these nightmares would never go away—that I would have to seek professional mental care in order to cope with these horrid images. I simply could not shake these scenes on my own.

So, at last, I collected my thoughts with the last shred of reserve I possessed, cleared my throat and started to speak. "You have a nerve sitting there telling me how you don't want to lose us, your life. This is also my life, remember, or have you conveniently forgotten that too? That was also my life, I should say. I thought you and I would be forever, that the bonds we shared were unbreakable. I thought our solid foundation could not be shaken or destroyed—that we, you and I, were a team, always standing back to back and protecting each other from the world. Fighting for us, for our sons, for our family… at least, this was what *I* always did. I thought you were on the same team, Chris. I thought we had a marriage, a partnership that was impenetrable…" My voice left me in the lurch and I simply could not go on. I was being choked by the emotion sticking in my throat. I could feel the tears pooling in my eyes.

He got up from where he sat and came over to me. He grabbed my upper arms in his hands to pull me to his chest.

I unfolded my arms and pulled away from him. I walked over to the window. He stayed at the desk where I left him, his arms hanging by his sides.

"Lilly," he looked at me helplessly, "just let me hold you. Please give me another chance. What can I do to make you understand that that woman from Cameroon was a mistake? It meant nothing to me. You are all I want. As a woman, as my lover, for God's sake, you are the mother of my sons. We have been together for forever, Lilly." He helplessly raked his fingers through his hair. He looked at me with desperation in his beautiful eyes.

This was about as much as I could take. I had let him speak and when I heard what he was saying, I was numbed by the shock. Could this be, the man I loved so deeply and respected so much, was this him speaking about someone he had been intimate with in this callous, uncaring, and cold way? How dared he simply diminish the contribution Ayanda made to his life? If it were not for her arriving on our doorstep with Sophie, I would still have been living in my own fool's paradise. I would be none the wiser of any of his antics.

This incident happened for a reason. What exactly the reason could be was totally obscured at this stage. I only experienced the pain. I was so convinced of the fact that this catastrophe had to have a deeper purpose. No one should go through such torment in vain. I was convinced I should merely try to cope as well as I could. Try to hold on to my sanity as best I could. The purpose would be unveiled at some point in the future.

I breathed deeply, closed my eyes, and counted to ten.

"Chris, please don't tax my patience. You contracted HIV because you slept around once too often. Your game of Russian roulette hopefully ended with Ayanda."

When he heard me saying this, he became quite pale and sat back down. He had that defiant look on his face.

He leaned his head back and closed his eyes. "What do you mean 'Russian roulette?'" He asked quietly.

Neither of us spoke. I kept looking at him but his eyes remained closed. Then he looked at me with defiance on his face. In this moment one of his favourite quotes repeated itself in my mind. He had said it so often during our life together. "Attack is the best defence. Never admit to any wrongdoing." He always told our sons this. I usually would get furious and countered him with "Gentlemen, always own up to your responsibility and take your punishment like a man."

I looked down at my hands. I rubbed over my nails, which used to be impeccably manicured but now were short and bare.

"The time for your fun and games and innocent looks has passed. Forever, I daresay, dear Chris. At least with me that is, I should add. It has come to my knowledge of how you fucked around behind my back all these years, dearest." I paused in order to get some air as it felt as though my heart might jump out of my throat. Then I continued, quietly. "You have effectively put an end to our life together. Surely you must realize that? Now that this can of worms has been opened, neither one of us can continue the same way we were in the past. I cannot fathom ever letting you touch me again. Do I still love you? Yes, I guess I do. The emotion I have for you is not something that can die so quickly. I will probably always love you. We shared so much, Chris. We had three sons together. Would I sacrifice myself for this emotion? Here, dear Chris, I have to say no. I have also done my fair share of thinking and I have come to the conclusion that I, as a person, need more. I need someone by my side whom I can respect and look up to."

I walked back to the sofa and sat down opposite him. He sat there quietly, looking at me, really listening to me. I continued in a normal tone of voice, which surprised me greatly as I felt as though I were totally coming apart, blabbering on incoherently as my mind could only follow one word at a time but from somewhere inside me, the words poured forth. They must have made sense somehow because Chris was actually listening to me. This was very unusual, as he would normally interrupt me constantly so as to state his point of view on almost everything I said.

"For the longest time I put our sons' and your needs above my own. I was always there for you, firstly, because I am, sorry, was your wife. I was always there for the boys because they are my children, and I love them more than life. I am their mother and always will be. Like you will always be their father. My own needs and whatever else I felt, I always pushed to the back, they were less important to me. Most of the time, what I wanted, I simply gave up on because it would not have fit into what the family wanted or what you wanted. So when Ayanda came and I heard about all the other women…"

At this he interrupted me, "How did you hear about the other women? It must be that stupid bitch friend of yours spreading rumours !"

Unbelievable as it may sound, he actually had the nerve to ask this idiotic question. Did he really expect an answer from me? I remained calm and did not even bat an eyelid. "Whoever told me is not important at this stage, Chris. I am forever thankful that I did find out, otherwise, I would still be living in that fool's paradise where I have been living for too long. I have done a tremendous amount of reflection. Where I am currently on my life's journey and where I would want to go—I have to tell you that you do not feature in any of my pictures of my future."

I fell silent and sat there looking at him. My hands quietly folded in my lap.

Chris sat opposite me. He was looking at the ground or staring at my feet—I was not sure which- his eyes were downcast. Neither one of us spoke.

He placed his hands with the fingertips exactly pressed together under his chin then he looked me in the eyes. He had moved forward on the chair and now sat looking at me like a predator ready to pounce. He reminded me of a praying mantis.

"So, Lilly, what is it that you want, exactly?" His voice sounded extraordinarily calm, albeit with a tone of sarcasm in it.

"I want a divorce." I had rehearsed this sentence so often in my mind the past couple of weeks but it was still an immense shock to hear me say it aloud. I had never imagined I would actually utter these words, ever!

Now Chris got up and walked over to the window. He was silent for a very long time before he spoke. "And besides the divorce, what else do you want?"

I kept looking at him. "I will not suffer because of your stupidity. You will leave this house and take your personal belongings with you. Everything in this house will remain exactly the way it is now. The boys will continue their university and schools exactly like before. You will continue to pay for their education. I will maintain my current lifestyle, and my allowance will be for my use only. For the upkeep of the property, the servants as well as the expenses with regard to the children, you will continue to be responsible."

He laughed sardonically. "You have the nerve, stupid cow, after all these years of living in the lap of luxury and never lifting a finger to help make all this possible, to demand from me—"

I interrupted him quietly. "Now, now, dearest, don't get spiteful. According to the divorce law in this country, I can sue for divorce on the grounds of infidelity or the fact that you have gone crazy. Don't challenge me. I have more than enough proof of your infidelity to hold up in a court of law. I will do it, Chris. Don't contest this and don't fight me on my demands either. You are well in a position financially to provide for our lives, to continue uninterrupted, without anyone suffering any discomfort. "

How I managed to sit there so calmly, I cannot explain. From somewhere I got the strength to speak clearly, my voice unfaltering and no sign of a tear in my eye at this stage.

He came to stand in front of me, his hands in his pockets. I met his gaze straight. "Lillian," Chris never called me this unless it was incredibly serious, "Lillian, I might die. Have you thought about that?"

The nerve! "Christian," I hardly ever called him by his full name unless it was very serious, "why is it that I am now the one who should be thinking of you dying? Don't you see the flaw in this picture? Did I bring this illness into this relationship? Did I go looking for adventure outside of the framework of this marriage? How come you suddenly want to make this disease my responsibility? You should have known better! You have lived with me here— you have seen the babies moving in and out of this house! You have exactly the same knowledge of this disease as I do. Yes, I feel sorry for you because I don't think you realized the consequences of what you were doing all these years. You did not ever imagine that your life, which you lived in the shadows, would ever become known to me or that you might lose everything you had. Well, now it all did happen that way and unfortunately you will lose the part of your life that was legit. Go on living your dark life—may it bring you all the happiness you could not find with me. I will have no part of it. I will not take care of you, remind you to take your medication, or do your laundry any longer. You are on your own from now on, my dear."

Having said this, I got up. I stood in front of him, our bodies no more than an inch apart. I looked him straight in the eye and repeated, "From now on, Christian, you are on your own." I stepped around him and made my way to the door where I paused, my hand on the handle. "I will have Selina pack the rest of your clothes. Send a driver around tomorrow to collect your things. As for being with the boys, arrange your meetings with them directly. Count me out of any of your get-togethers." Then I opened the door, left, and closed it silently behind me. I continued walking steadily, not halting anywhere, and controlling myself not to break into a run, until I reached my bedroom. I entered, locked the door and fell onto the bed with my face buried in the pillows and sobbed my heart out. Thank goodness for many goose down pillows which effectively smothered the sounds of my heart wrenching sobs.

I have no recollection of how long I lay there. I must have fallen asleep because I eventually woke up with a start. It took me a minute to realize it was actually a knock at the door that woke me up.

I sat up, stroked down my hair and tried to look as collected as I could. I got up to unlock the door and went back to my bed.

"Come in," I called with make-believe happiness in my voice.

The door opened and in came my three sons. Connor carried a tray with a huge pile of buttered toast and four mugs from which the aroma of tea and honey drifted. They came in in silence, Connor placed the tray in the middle of my bed, and they sat down. Chris, Jr. so close to my right that he was actually touching me, Christopher to my left but at a distance, and Connor sat down near the foot of the bed.

At first no one spoke. I was a bit bewildered having just woken up, the emotional exhaustion evident on my face. I could feel the boys looking at me. I must look a mess because I could see the pitiful look on Connor's face.

"Mom," he began and then fell silent again.

"Mom," he started again. "Dad spoke to us." Silence. I did not say anything. I merely sat there looking from the one to the other. Then I leaned forward and handed each one their mug with their name on it. I took mine along with a slice of toast, passing the plate around to Chris, Jr., Christopher, and Connor. Each one took a slice. There was silence while we ate.

"So your father spoke to you," I said at last. "What did he say to you?"

Christopher answered me. "He said he's moving out." He leaned forward and took another piece of toast. He never looked at me once as he spoke.

Chris, Jr. chipped in. "He said you're really, really mad at him, and he will not be living with us anymore." I looked at him and I could see the confusion in his eyes. Trust his father to swing all of this in his own favour and make me responsible for all of it.

"Guys, listen to me. Your father and I have decided to separate. This will mean that he will no longer be living here in this house. It does not mean that you will not see him again. He is and will always and forever be your dad. He loves you as before, and you will still be doing all the things with him exactly as you did before."

"Where are you going?" Chris, Jr. was looking at me with a very worried expression on his face.

"I am going nowhere. I am living here in this house exactly as I have always done. This is our home. This is where you guys grew up, and this will always be your home for as long as you want to come back here. Nothing is changing. You will still continue your education at your school, Chris, as will you, Christopher, and you, Connor, will still go to varsity as before. Nothing will change as far as your lifestyle is concerned. Your father and I still expect of you to do your best. Nothing will ever change as far as that is concerned. You are still expected to behave in a proper manner. The only difference will be that your father will not be living with us any longer."

There was silence.

Christopher looked at me, took a sip of tea, and asked, "Why did he leave?"

I looked down. I could not bring myself to answer. These are my sons. How could I tell them that their father betrayed their mother while he was always preaching fidelity to the boys? How could I now destroy the image of their hero in their eyes? Would I be believable to them if I omit the truth, simply tell them a story? Two of them are now men with girlfriends of their own. How will it influence and affect them if I should tell them that their father, who always sounded so convinced of what was right or wrong, had committed the greatest betrayal of all? That he himself did not know which path was the right one to choose in moments of weakness?

I waited a long time before I lifted my eyes to meet their questioning ones. All eyes directed on poor little me, expectation in all of them.

I owe it to my sons to tell them the truth. That they should know that sometimes even people we love very much make mistakes. I read somewhere once in another lifetime that it is not the problems we face in life which are important but the way in which we solve those problems. We, as a family are facing the worst crisis any family could face and we have to find a way out of this situation which will be dignified and responsible. I will tell them in the softest kindest way possible.

"Sometimes people find they are no longer compatible after the longest time of being together. They find that they have grown apart, and they do not share the same principles and interests any longer. They find that they have different ideas about the most important things in life. In such a case, if these different ideas become irreconcilable, then it is better for all concerned to split and live apart." I paused and took a deep breath of air. "Your father has contracted HIV..................."Silence. Shock and disgust on Christopher's face, incomprehension and confusion on Christian Jr's. Connor stared at the cup in his hands." I continue " We are civilized," I had to pause here and breathe deeply, "and your father and I have three stunning sons together. Strong and principled young men. Look at the three of you, you are magnificent examples of the species. Your father and I are incredibly proud of you. We will always be your parents...No, he will not die. You all know about the AIDS babies I temporarily take care of and you all know about the medicines available. With the proper care and if he takes good care of himself, he will be absolutely fine..."

I looked at Chris, Jr., "and I am still going to give you a kiss in front of the school when I drop you off or pick you up." I smiled at him and hugged him close and it broke the seriousness of the moment.

"Aw, Mom!" He groaned, "It is embarrassing!"

Christopher chipped in, "She did the same to Connor and me, bro, why should it be different with you?"Christopher spoke softly but I could pick up on the emotion in his voice. He refrained from making any comment with regards to the devastating news I just delivered. I guess they wanted to be strong for me. Christopher and Connor must realize how much agony and torment I must be going through as a wife and as a mother.

Connor smiled and sipped his tea. "Chris, our mother is a great lady. Just imagine if she never gave you a kiss. She could have been boring like some of the other moms from school." He looked at his brothers and the bond amongst them was very apparent. Each one so incredibly different in nature and yet so very alike. I felt like gathering them in my arms and holding them close.

So we sat there on my bed talking about things we did together as a family, naming things they would still like to do together, and reminiscing anecdotes from the past. In this moment I knew we were going to be all right. My children and I would survive this crisis because we were together, and we would support each other. Amongst themselves the boys could have different opinions but the very moment that one of them faced an adverse situation, the other two lined up behind their brother in solidarity.

We were, after all, a family, and Chris and I have raised them well. The basic principles to support and respect one another, to stand as one, and face difficulties of life as a unity shine through. Even though Chris was not physically present in this circle, he was very much visible. These were his sons. I would never do anything to ever diminish the role he had to play in their lives or the influence he should have as an example of a father.

Preparing for a divorce is a horrid affair. Those who have gone through it do not even wish it upon their enemies. The emotional turmoil makes one act completely irrational; the fears, which develop during this period, are both illogical and unnatural.

No matter how calm and collected I appeared to be, I realized the horrific tension once I sat in the courtroom with the other party on the opposite side of the room. To say I hated Chris would be exaggerated—to say that he left me absolutely cold, would be accurate. To hate is to imply there is some sort of feeling left whereas the coldness, this abstract disinterest I felt toward him, meant he was simply another human being sharing this planet with me. I could not even fathom having had three children fathered by him. What type of person had I been to have let that happen? Still, the best thing that had happened in my life was the fact that I had my sons.

After that blissful morning with my boys sitting around me after Chris left, I had not seen him at all. For visits with the boys, well, he contacted them directly. Chris, Jr. usually got picked up straight from school on Fridays and dropped at our gate on Sunday afternoon.

There had been one holiday since then when Chris took Christopher and Chris, Jr. with him to Europe. He went for business, and then they spent a few days at a theme park outside Paris. It was raining, and, according to Chris, Jr., they had a very miserable time as he got a cold but his father told him to behave like a man and not be sick and whining like a sissy.

I never asked but Chris, Jr. volunteered the information that his father was alone. No woman accompanying him. He also mentioned on a few occasions what they did on the weekends he visited his father. He never mentioned a woman. Honestly, I tried not to think about it. I simply counted myself lucky to have come out of this affair with my health intact.

Not a day went by that I did not thank my lucky stars, all the angels and the saints for the fact I came out of this real life thriller in healthy condition. I cannot imagine what it must be like to know that that virus is alive and simply waiting for the system to show weakness in order to break out with all the ferocity of a bushfire to destroy the human body. There are so many amazing people whose spirit live on strong while their bodies simply waste away, eaten up from the inside. Parents, with dependent children, who are simply physically not capable. The tragedy—that is HIV—cannot be comprehended by someone who has not seen it and dealt with it like I have, the poor babies I cared for occasionally, who had no part in it and yet suffered because of their parents' carelessness. The reality of what Chris faced every morning when he woke up, I tried not to think about it. I tried not to start feeling sorry for him or to have compassion for him. I was afraid I would become soft, forgive him, and take him back. Should his immune system fail at some stage, he would need care as he would not be able to take care of himself. This is no simple influenza virus. I have cared for the wasted little people who passed through my home before being placed in specialized orphanages. I have seen horrific suffering. I would not want to see it happen to someone I once cared for very deeply.

So there we sat in the courtroom. Me on one side with my lawyer and his assistant—he brought her along just for the off chance she would have to jump up and run to find evidence of precedents in the law library. My lawyer, who himself had personally been the victim, so to speak, of four marriages, was not taking any chances. It was going to be a very bitter fight. I was dressed in white. White is considered by some tribes of this world, as the colour of mourning. So I wore white. I had wasted so many good years of my life on that man, it was proper that I mourn those years of being the faithful wife.

How was it possible that the immense love I thought I once felt for him could have vanished like mist before the hot African sun? I amazed myself, and I felt ashamed at times. Did I still feel anger? Was it anger that blinded me and made me felt like the love was gone? This maelstrom of feelings wrenched its way through my mind a million times a day, all the waking hours. My mind would start running all by itself. When I could eventually pull my wits about me, I was shaking and terribly anxious.

Chris looked thinner but still dashingly handsome and gorgeous coming through the door with his lawyer and her assistant. *How appropriate that his lawyer is a woman,* I thought. *Maybe he had slept with her.* I wonder if she knew about his infection. *Would he be telling his new conquests about it? How many had there been since Ayanda? Had he phoned them up, invited them for a drink, and, shortly after placing the order for martinis, casually slipped the words "By the way I am HIV positive"?*

Chris came over to our table, walked up to me, and held out his hand.

"Good morning, Mrs. Johnston. You look ravishing as always." He took my hand kissed it on the back whilst looking into my eyes, smiled, placed my hand back on the table and went over to his side.

If I weren't already sitting, I would have needed a chair at this point.

I was still reeling from this encounter when the "All rise" was called and the judge entered the courtroom.

The judge did not look at any of us. She came in as though she was in a hurry. We were the first on the list for the day and, if her body language was anything to go by, she had many cases to get through for the day. What seemed like such a momentous event in my life was, to her, no more than a numbered case in her very busy day.

Her name was Judy. I have met her on some occasions at social functions. Johannesburg is like a fishpond in which all the colourful big koi fishes always bumped into one another all the time. I could not remember her surname but I remembered she was a very well-respected judge with excellent connections coming from a most influential tribe controlling mines in the north of the country. As far as I could remember, she had four children, all of them living abroad, but no one ever spoke about her husband and no one ever dared to ask either. So, even though she was tough and revered, she had a friendly smile in her eyes when she did look at me over the rim of her glasses. If she recognized me, she did not show any signs of it.

The case was stated and proceedings began.

I tried to keep calm, letting my lawyer do the talking as I was told. I kept my eyes focused on the floor in front of our table and my hands firmly clasped in my lap until I lost all feeling in my fingers. There were moments when I stole a glance at Chris. He looked pale, his jaws clenched, he had his hands intertwined on top of the table. Once our eyes met. He looked at me as though to say, "You started this madness." His lips looked thin and bloodless. I felt, at times, as though I should jump up and put an end to this reality. We had been married for a lifetime! How could I allow such a thing as a divorce? People are supposed to be married "in sickness and in health, for richer for poorer, good times and bad times till death us do part." According to the vows we took: "Let no man pull apart what I have brought together." But then the adult in me spoke the rationale that I had kept my part of the bargain. It was Chris who'd forsaken his vows. Is it not true about the partnership which is called marriage that if one partner is not happy and content, then they should talk about the problem and try to solve it? Chris accused me of not being understanding, of revelling in my position as "Mrs. Johnston" as he said, and forgetting him in the process. Weird story and an even more bizarre reason to justify infidelity according to my set of values. But, now we were here in this courtroom, and, of course, I was not going to stand up and call off this divorce hearing.

After four hours of lawyers constantly bickering, interrupting one another, called to order, fighting about payments and support, the judge called it a day and made her decision. I was bewildered and at this point I did not trust myself to speak or to comment, and I was not even too sure that I understood English anymore so I merely rose when the judge left the courtroom.

Chris stayed seated with his lawyer leaning over toward him. Softly talking. I could not make out what she was saying to him but I could see he was not happy.

"What will be the outcome of all of this, Adam?" I asked softly of my lawyer.

He looked at me with gentle eyes. "The judge awarded you all your conditions, Lilly. She cut down a bit on the amount, which we claimed for you personally, but we expected it anyway, and so I had asked for slightly more than you wanted. So actually, you should be dancing and singing now, my girl. You have been successfully divorced." He held his arms open and I moved to give him a hug.

"Thank you, Adam," I whispered, resting my cheek against his.

At this moment, Chris looked my way. The expression in his eyes were like death. No emotion, no warmth, nothing. He mouthed the word "bitch," then looked away.

That was the last time I saw Chris—that morning in the courtroom with him mouthing, "bitch" and looking away. He never contacted me again. It was as though the past twenty odd years never happened, except for the fact that there were three young men who bore testimony to the fact that these years did happen.

I left the courtroom with Adam and we were driven back to his offices. I got out of his car and got into mine. All mechanical. I drove home and when I got to my house, I could not remember that I had driven there. I parked the car and sat behind the steering wheel. Just sat there. Selina came out because she heard the car. She stood on the patio looking at me for a long time, then she came to the car, opened my door, and took my hand.

"Shame, shame, shame, mama," she said. Then she led me up the steps, into the house, up the staircase to my bedroom to my bed. She made me sit on the edge of the bed and took off my shoes. Then she fluffed my pillows and made me lie down. My bed was freshly made with the white bedding I liked so much. I only ever used white bedding and, immediately, I thought, *What a bizarre habit and an even more incredulous thing to think about now.*

Then I started crying. At first it was a soft crying, and then I waled and howled.

Selina left the room, not saying a word, but a very short time later, Janice showed up. She came in with a tray with tea and sandwiches on it, closed the door behind her, kicked off her shoes, and got on the bed with me. She lay next to me, holding my hand, not speaking while I merely waled, whimpered and cried.

I went into mourning. I mourned my marriage and the loss of my husband. I mourned my life as part of a couple. Suddenly, I was a person living on the edge of society. As is typical in such a case, many hostesses were not inviting me to social events any longer, as I was now single and therefore a threat to their own liaisons or marriages. I suddenly came to realize that, in reality, no marriage or partnership was really secure and that people were always looking for the next magnet to be attracted to. I became cynical. Did "love" really exist? Was it not merely a result of women's imagination? The same thread of fiction as believing that each one on this earth is special?

I questioned everything in my life. I developed an irrational fear of death. I was suspicious of everyone who rang the bell at my gate, convinced that I would be murdered brutally in my home. Sleeplessness was a constant companion, and I became so sleep deprived that I was hallucinating.

With the help of Janice, Selina took over the running of my home entirely. The two of them arranged the shopping, the fetching of Chris, Jr. in the mornings, and picking him up again after school. Selina saw to it I was being cared for like a baby. She switched off my mobile phone and became my secretary, taking messages, and getting Janice to call back on my behalf. I stayed in bed, sometimes sitting and staring aimlessly out the window, going downstairs and sitting in the library behind Chris' desk. In the days following the divorce, Selina packed up all his things according to a list that was delivered to the house by a messenger from Chris' lawyer's office. Due to this fact, the study looked bare. Bookshelves were now empty what with all his books on mining, geology, and gemstones gone. The beautiful maps which were adorning the walls were also gone but one could clearly see where they had hung as the panelling was darker, bearing evidence to their having been in one spot for many, many years. I would just sit behind the desk. Existing. Merely being.

Then, one fine morning, I woke up and stretched, got out of bed, padded to the window, drew back my beautiful drapes and thought, *What a spectacular day.*

I went downstairs to the kitchen. Selina was there preparing Chris, Jr.'s breakfast and school snack. She turned around at the sound of me entering the kitchen. She looked at me, pushed her glasses higher on her nose, and smiled.

"Eish, mama, you are up early," she said.

"Morning, Gogo. Yes, I feel great. Is Chris, Jr. awake already?"

"No, but he will be happy to see you for a change. I make coffee while you call him." At this she turned back to finishing what she was doing.

I went to Chris' bedroom. He was completely tangled in his duvet, sleeping across the bed with the pillows on the floor and homework books still open on his desk. No matter how many times I have told him to pack his bookcase the night before, he still did it in a terrible rush in the morning with the result that many a time he had forgotten a book at home somewhere on his desk. I smiled. I thought, *Who cares? I am alive and I have my children and telling chil-*

dren what to do is part of being a mom's life, never mind that I have to tell him every day because soon he'll be gone and then I will miss him terribly.

It was as though my thoughts or my presence woke him up. He turned on his side, frowned as he looked unseeingly at me. Then he focused and said "Hi, Mom. Will you take me to school today?"

"Yes, darling," I said. "Time to get moving. I'll see you in the kitchen."

The Lessons We Learn

I was drawn back to the present by the announcement of the airhostess that we were about to land at Oliver Tambo International Airport in Johannesburg, South Africa. A soft touch on my shoulder and a smiling face reminded me to fasten my seatbelt and place my chair back in the upright position. These days one was not allowed to call them anything else but flight attendants. It was apparently discriminating. In South Africa everything was discriminating against someone somewhere, one had to really watch what one said. No one was dumb anymore; people became "intellectually challenged" in stead.

Many years have passed since that morning when we, my boys and I, sat on my bed, talking. I can still remember we sat like that for the greater part of the day. In a way, the boys were reluctant to leave me. All of us wanted to remain close. To draw the assurance that our secure world—the world they had known all their lives—would remain intact. I needed their presence as much as they needed mine. I knew I had to be the one to determine the way forward. I was the one to support them as the adult, and a mother always took care of her children.

My boys have remained as attached and close to each other over the years as they had been when they were little. Even though great distances had separated them over the past couple of years, they always took the time to visit one another and spend special time alone together. The three of them got together somewhere in this beautiful world—no girls or other friends allowed. They went scuba diving, camping on the beach, somewhere in the Bush-veld to do animal trekking on foot, so many great adventures I was sometimes jealous.

They have all flown my nest now. But they are like swallows—they all return to me for the summer to my beach cottage on a long stretch of beach on my island in the Caribbean. Of course it is not "my" island in the way it sounds, simply that I had talked about one day living on that island ever since I could remember. When Chris, Jr. left Africa to attend university abroad, I left too. Even though the Caribbean is now my home, and it is breathtak-ingly, exquisitely beautiful, the African sunset and the smell of the earth after the rain is what is constantly missing in my life, and sometimes the memories cause me to cry with the loss of it.

My life has undergone dramatic changes in the past fifteen years. My hair is completely white, and my face is soft with wrin-kles that I had to befriend over the years. They would not be coaxed away with any amount of serum, cream, or massage, let alone makeup. My figure is femininely rounded, as Antonio says, with curves that fit perfectly into his hands. What a great way to describe overweight!

I trust people upfront; they no longer have to prove they are trustworthy. I wear spectacles that permanently hang on a chain of pearls around my neck. My arms finally became too short for me to read without the help of these blasted glasses.

And then there is Antonio. My Antonio. A man who is my haven from the world. No matter how bad it is, when I have shared it with him, everything suddenly becomes downsized, and he helps me to find a solution to any situation I face. He is a research scien-tist and ten years my senior. Wise, soft-spoken, unpretentious, and, yet, when he walks into a room, people turn to look. One feels authority emanating from him without him trying to enforce it. I can communicate with him without saying a word. He is my soul mate. He taught me to love myself as I was and not as I wanted to be. To face reality and to accept me the person I am and that it was okay to be that way. That he loved me exactly as I am.

Looking back, I clearly see the arrival of Ayanda and Sophie in our lives as the catalyst that was needed to save my own life. I have discovered myself in so many different ways: who I really am deep inside, what I like, and truly dislike. Once Chris left, I grieved his departure and the death of our life together. I gave myself the time to grieve. I became like a hermit. There were weeks on end when I would only occasionally leave the house to take Chris, Jr. to school and fetch him again. Grocery shopping was done by Janice or on the Internet.

Society was red hot with all the gossip in the beginning. At first there were phone calls from "friends" trying to fish for information about what really happened. I would simply be noncommittal, and when they realized that there were no answers forthcoming, they stopped calling. There is a saying that one really recognizes who one's true friends are when one experiences a life's crisis. Take my word—it's true.

Janice was the only one whom I would phone, and Janice and her family were the only people whom I would invite to my home during that period. She was there to wipe my cheeks when the tears flowed like rivers, she quietly listened, offering no advice but only holding me close. She listened when I wanted to talk and just sat with me when the words stopped.

And here I am on my way back to attend the funeral of the man I once thought I loved more than life itself. I never saw Chris again after that morning in the court all those years ago. Our respective lawyers handled the formalities, papers were signed in lawyers' offices, and monies got transferred. Honestly, everything happened without a hitch. I never asked the boys any questions about their father, and they seldom volunteered any information. I respected that. When he was younger, Chris, Jr. would occasionally tell me what happened over weekends but as he grew older, he ceased this practice, and if I asked what they did, he would answer with, "Oh, Mom, many things. I can't remember all now." I did not pry. I guess it was his way to politely tell me to mind my own business.

Chris and I continued to live our lives as though we never knew each other. I had often wondered how it could have been that I lived intimately with the man. I thought I knew him as well as I knew myself and then everything came undone afterwards. Until Antonio taught me that no one ever really knows what is in the heart of someone—even if you live with that person for a very long time. It's impossible to know someone completely, because we are all separated individuals.

In reality, we are all alone, and we are all loners. Only you, as a person, can know what's in your heart. Someone else might think they know, but they can never tell for certain. It took me a long time to forgive myself for not knowing, for not reading the signs, for not being more careful and observant. No one has x-ray knowledge—we are not divine creatures. So, I let it go.

I accepted my life exactly as it happened, and I managed to nurture a soft spot for Chris. He suffered enough as it was. I imagined that somewhere deep down, he felt really sorry he'd destroyed the beautiful life we had together. But then, it was a beautiful life only from my point of view. Maybe to him, it was a miserable existence. Maybe that was why he went looking for liaisons with other women. Something was lacking in his life, and he did not have the ability to communicate this to me. Of course, if he really ever felt sorry, I would now never know. We never ever spoke again, not even a phone call on birthdays, Christmastime, or Easter. Not a single phone call as a means of good wishes or congratulations. I simply let it be.

So it came to this. Chris died in a car crash. He was alone. He was drunk. He was going incredibly fast and according to Janice, the car became airborne and there simply was no way he could control it. He apparently did not suffer. His neck was broken and he died instantly. It was middle of the day local time when the phone call came. Antonio and I were lying down for our regular siesta in the hammocks. The sea is twenty metres from a shady place where we take a siesta every day.

It was close to midnight in Africa. Anton called me. His comforting voice sounded concerned over the line that connected us across many thousands of kilometers. He and his wife were regular visitors here at my beach cottage. They came every year in May, when the winter started to settle over the Highveld.

"Hello, Lilly. How are you?" I knew from the way he sounded this was not a courtesy call.

"I am fine, thanks, Anton. How are you? Why do you sound so strange?" In my mind I was frantic—the boys are fine, I spoke to them the day before and no one was near Africa. Janice was living in Cape Town and was healthy and well—that would leave only Anton and his wife Jenny."

He ignored my question, "Is Antonio with you?"

"Yes, yes, he is here."

"Lilly," his voice sounded tired, "I am afraid I am the bearer of bad news." I imagined him sitting down, taking off his glasses, wiping his face and his eyes, then putting his glasses back on his nose. There were even permanent dents on the side of his nose where the glasses always came to rest.

"Go on," I said, my heart beating in my throat.

"Chris died earlier this evening."

I lay back down on my hammock. Antonio was beside me holding my hand.

"What happened, Anton?"

"Car accident, Lilly. Chris' love of speed and all things fast took him away."

"Where did it happen?" I asked.

"On the north coast. The hospital notified me. As his physician, he had my details on him." A pause. I could not think of anything to say. I did not even feel the tears rise.

"Was it sudden, Anton, did he suffer?"

"No, Lilly, according to the physician it was instant." I did not know what to say.

"Lilly, I just wanted to say I'll take care of all the arrangements. Chris shared with me the details of his funeral a long time ago. He wanted to be cremated so I will arrange this."

"Thanks, Anton." I paused and looked into Antonio's concerned face. He was holding my free hand in both of his and stroking over the back of my hand softly with his thumbs. "I will obviously be there for the ceremony. I will let you know about my flight arrangements." Then I simply hung up on him.

We remained sitting like this. Not talking, merely sitting close to each other. Antonio put his arm around my shoulder. There was nothing to say. For me it was a silent closure of that chapter of my life that had Chris as a main character. So we sat, gently swinging to and fro with our bare feet touching the beautiful soft sand, and stared out to sea. Every now and then, Antonio planted a kiss on my forehead and stroked my cheek.

In the early hours of the evening, with the sky changing colours and the water coming higher up on the beach, we went inside. That evening we did not dine at home but we went to a cozy restaurant down the road. The owner, Rosita, was my age. She had a very large family and even more grandchildren, and it was always a joyous occasion to go there.

We arranged our arrivals in such a way that the boys would meet me at the airport. We would then go to the hotel together. Connor flew in from London and brought his charming wife along. She was an investment banker and tough as nails. She operated with three mobile phones, and she scared me, but, as Antonio kept telling me, I did not have to live with her. Connor was a partner at a prestigious plastic surgery practice and so, I guess, they suited each other perfectly.

Christopher flew in from Japan. He was doing his doctorate in Japanese, of all things, a language and a culture so incredibly different and completely opposite from all we were accustomed to in the West. Christopher had been living at some sort of institution somewhere on a hillside in the middle of a forest now for some years already. He meditates, he has long hair (clean at least), and he has the most peaceful aura about him.

Chris, Jr., a geologist like his father, flew in from Argentina. His curly hair too long for my liking, crinkles around his eyes when he smiled (which was often), and a body to kill for was still a bit of a playboy. He came alone as, quite frankly, he would have been spoiled for choice of which gorgeous girlfriend to bring along. He was somewhere off the coast of South America on an oilrig when I called him about his father.

I cleared customs, picked up my luggage and headed out to meet my boys.

We stayed at a most beautiful hotel near the heart of the busy Sandton business district. This sanctuary was secure like anything you could imagine with gardens, indigenous African trees, and a swimming pool, which resembled a lake.

That night, at the dinner table, we spoke easily enough about what was happening in our lives. Each one had so much to tell. Then we moved outside, to a quiet table with candlelight and torches marking the murmuring stream next to it.

Chris started speaking about the time when they were little, then Christopher chipped in and before long they had us rolling with anecdotes about their childhood, what they did (some of this I never even knew and I was really grateful I did not know at the time it happened). They spoke about their father. India, Connor's wife, was with us and she laughed until the tears were streaming down her face. We sat there, laughing and crying and then, close to three o'clock in the morning, India placed her hand on Connor's arm and said, "Darling, I do hope, Junior will not be as mischievous as you lot one day." He turned to look at her and the look in their eyes took my breath away.

"Excuse me, which junior are you talking about?" I asked.

Connor took her hand in both of his and looked at me. "Mom, we actually wanted a better moment to tell you," he paused, looked back at her and smiled, then he looked at each of his brothers and then back at me and continued "India, I mean, we, are expecting a baby."

I jumped up at this and went around the table to lock both of them in an embrace.

"My children, congratulations," I sobbed. "You could not have picked a better moment to share this wonderful news with all of us. Oh, I am so happy! Thank you for telling me in person like this. Oh my God! I am going to be a grandmother!"

There we were again, my boys, me, this wonderfully intelligent woman who was going to be the mother of my first grandchild, all of us bonding, revelling in the fact that we were family, we were close, and we loved one another. And that, as a family, we would stand strong—we would take care of one another.

Chris was laid to rest in the same cemetery as Sophie, albeit in another section where the urns got put into a special wall. The flowers for Chris were delivered by a florist directly to the place he was to be interred. She left a huge bouquet of white roses bound with a pink satin ribbon for me.

After the ceremony, I took Christian junior's hand in my left and Christopher's hand in my right. I gave Connor the bouquet to carry.

"Gentlemen, I want you to come with me," I said.

Connor and India walked behind us. "Where to, Mom?" Connor asked. "Where are we going with these flowers?"

I kept silent. "You'll see."

The trees that lined the path had grown tall over the past sixteen years but memory served me well, and we ended up in front of a small grave with a white alabaster cherub guarding the grave. I took the bouquet and placed it on the marble slab.

The boys were silent while they read the inscription.

Christopher spoke first, "Sophie Johnston. She died sixteen years ago." He looked at me enquiringly, "I did not know we had a sister? Who was she, Mom?"

I looked at him, closed my eyes, made the sign of the cross and smiled. I placed my left arm over Christian's arm on my left and my right arm over Christopher's on my right with Connor and India walking behind us and we walked out of the cemetery toward the waiting limo.

"Now boys, I have to tell you a story. It all happened a very long time ago here in Africa."

Made in the USA
Middletown, DE
31 January 2024